pretty
AND
reckless

CHARITY FERRELL

a note from the author

Dear Reader,

This story may contain trigger warnings to some such as sexual assault, and discussions about rape and suicide.

one

ELISE

"Thanks," I said, grabbing the cup from the barista in my glove-covered hand and taking a seat in the back of the coffee shop. The Chicago winter draft spilled over me each time the frosted door opened and another customer piled in.

Settling in my seat, I draped my coat along the back of the chair next to me and brought the cup to my lips. The sweet liquid scorched the tip of my tongue before I quickly swallowed it down.

Peppermint, yum.

The table was sticky under my elbows, and I tucked my chin into the palm of my hand. Customers scurried around the shop, spilling creamer and sprinkling sugar into their cups hurriedly. They bumped into each other with no apologies as they struggled to make it to work on time. A few sat at tables, positioned in front of their laptops, oblivious to the chaos surrounding them with the help of their headphones. Two middle-aged men transferred documents back and forth with heated faces and firm voices.

1

Then, there was me—the loner with no headphones, no computer, and nobody.

These people—the ones scurrying, studying, arguing—they were all living.

Me? I was just *there*. Just surviving.

I looked away from the men when they caught me staring, and that was when I saw him. I jerked my head back, scanned the shop, and then glanced back in his direction.

He was still there.

Why would he be here?

I couldn't tear my eyes away from him, and he became the new focus of my attention. He brushed melted snowflakes from his disarrayed amaretto curls before shaking them out while waiting in line. Taking off his glasses, he cleaned them and shoved them back up his nose. He wore a faded, dark green flannel shirt that peeked out from underneath his bulky coat and a thick neck scarf.

His actions weren't entertaining in the least, but for some reason, I couldn't tear my eyes away from him. Even though we'd only met once, I never forgot a face—especially one I wanted to smack. Three years ago, he'd studied me like a project he'd be graded on.

I was not a project.

I was not here for people's amusement.

In anger, I did what I did best—figured out a way to get him to leave me alone ... and screwed him over in the process. I'd destroyed his career, and he knew it was my fault. He had to hate me, and I didn't blame him.

The barista received a friendly grin when it was his turn to order, and he slipped a few bills in the tip jar. She handed him his coffee, an extra smile on the side, and he thanked her. The guy was too friendly—another reason I didn't like him. I didn't trust friendly. People weren't friendly for no reason. There was always an ulterior motive.

I took another sip of my latte.

Should I say something?

Hell no, absolutely not.

I needed to glance down and study the table until he left. It'd be too weird if he noticed me. The man knew too much—where I'd been and what I'd gone through. Whether he believed that information was a different story, but he knew.

"Elise."

My eyes flew up at the sound of my name. He stood in front of me with a matching smile of what he'd given the barista. I stared at him, our eyes locking, and waited to see where he was going with this, silently praying it would not be his drink in my face.

Scorch my face for scorching his career.

Fair trade.

"I thought it was you," he finally said, breaking our uncomfortable silence.

"Yeah, it's me," I replied awkwardly, setting my cup down.

I'd never run into someone from *there*. I had been sent five hours away for that very reason. My father wanted me far enough so that people wouldn't recognize me, but close enough that he could still choke me with his leash if I made a run for it.

My father also lied about where I was to other people. I was away, visiting my grandmother—who was actually living six feet under—or I was studying abroad. Given my reputation, I doubted people had believed him. He tried his hardest to keep our family name clean while I fought my hardest to trash it.

I was Elise Parks—the slutty, out-of-control heir to Chicago's most prominent entrepreneur. I was that girl who couldn't keep her legs closed, her hand absent of a drink, or her bloodstream clean of narcotics.

3

I wore trouble like a crown, and I wore it proud.

My infamy had begun on my fourteenth birthday after I raided my father's liquor cabinet with my best friend, Holly. After we were good and drunk, we decided it was a stellar idea to do cartwheels down the street. The cops were called, and we were taken away in handcuffs, neither one of us scared.

It delighted me when my father charged into the police station with a stricken face filled with embarrassment. His outrage and the backlash I received were music to my ears. Seeing him so unhappy was enough incentive to continue doing stupid shit for revenge.

But getting older, I had tried to break away from that role. I now had *some* power over my life. I'd decided it was time to move forward but cleaning up your reputation was harder than spitting on it.

He raised a brow. "What are you doing in Chicago?"

I took a drink before answering him. "I live here. What are you doing here?"

He curled his fingers around the edge of the chair as he leaned into it. "Me too. I just moved here to be closer to my family."

"Sounds like fun," I muttered.

Did he tell them what I said? Was he threatened?

"As fun as my job can be." He chuckled. "So, tell me, how have you been?"

I shrugged. "I haven't popped any pills recently. I've been clean for a few years, and I'm a legal adult, so I can spread my legs to whoever I please." I smiled smugly. "So, I'd say, I'm doing pretty damn well."

He scowled, telling me he was still as uptight as he had been when we first met.

"Okay, sorry." I held up my hand and delivered a look of innocence. "I've been on my best behavior, Doctor."

He shifted back on his heels and unhooked his fingers from the chair. "I'm glad to hear that. I expect never to see you there again?"

My back stiffened as my fingers tingled against my cup. "You still work there?"

His gaze dropped to his wet boots. "Yes, a few days a week until they find a replacement for me." The awkwardness grew until he broke it with the clap of his hands. "So, never again, deal?"

"Never say never," I grumbled.

Doing my best to stay out of trouble meant handing my father more control and allowing him to cut away what little self-dignity I had left. I gave up speaking my truth for freedom. That being said, I wasn't sure how long my exemplary behavior would last. Trouble always had a way of knocking on my door. I wasn't a methodical thinker. I was irrational and careless.

Fucked up people did fucked up things.

It was in our fucked up nature.

"I'm an optimist." He set his cup down, pulled out his wallet, plucked out a card, and slid it my way. "Here's my card. Call me if you ever find yourself in trouble or want to talk."

I looked from the card to him, eyeing him suspiciously, and a loud ringing came from his pocket.

What's his motive?

He fished out his phone from his jeans, glanced at the screen, and silenced the call. "It's my sister. I promised to babysit." Tapping his fingers against the table, he added, "Stay out of trouble," over his shoulder before turning to leave.

Before grabbing the card, I waited for the bell to ring at his departure.

Dr. Weston Snyder.

I glanced at the overflowing trash can, piled with empty cups.

5

Should I toss it?

Playing with the card in my hand, I was conflicted about whether to keep it.

Finally, I threw it into my purse.

And thank God I did.

two

ELISE

EIGHTEEN HOURS LATER

My decision-making rights needed to be revoked. Every choice I made in life was the wrong one. Pandemonium crept around me, following me like a shadow, and waited for every opportunity to sweep in and destroy my life more.

I cursed myself for my situation—crouched down and hiding in an abandoned alley at three in the morning with snow up to my ankles. My eye was swollen, my lip busted, and who knew what else was wrong with me. I was a hot mess. I took a timid glance to my left and then to my right, making sure the man chasing me wasn't anywhere nearby.

I cringed when I noticed the dried-up blood caked underneath my fresh manicure as I opened my Gucci clutch. It took a few attempts, but I finally got the clasp open with my shaking hands.

As I rifled through my belongings, my father's arrogant

voice rang through my ears, magnifying my headache. *"The only things open at three in the morning are legs, baby girl."*

I hate when he's right.

I shoved away a wad of cash, a tube of lipstick, and a pair of backup panties before finding my phone. The screen shone bright as I unlocked it.

I had five missed calls from Oliver.

Ignoring his call, I scrolled through my Contacts list and struggled to focus with one working eye while hitting Holly's name.

Pick up. Pick up.

I cried out in frustration when it went straight to voice mail. *Fuck!* I loved the girl, but she never kept her phone on.

It was probably a blessing in disguise that she hadn't answered. She was most likely with her boyfriend, and considering he was Oliver's best friend, it wouldn't have been very smart on my part to tell her where I was.

Glaring at the full moon, I cursed.

What can I do?

Who can I call to rescue me?

Certainly not my father.

I didn't have any other friends.

What happened that morning dawned on me.

My stomach twisted at the thought of calling *him*—an admission that I'd been full of shit at the coffee shop about changing for the better. My resources were limited, and he was my only hopeful option unless I wanted to land a pretty spot smack dab in tomorrow's blogs. With a breath of courage, I hit a name I never expected to dial.

"Hello?"

His voice was tired. I felt bad for waking him up and dragging him into my mess.

"Weston?" I croaked out.

"Yes?" His question was laced with confusion. Since he didn't have my number, he probably thought he was being drunk-dialed by some old fling.

"It's Elise." I shuddered while brushing my stiff fingers over my throat, skimming them across the deep scratches in my skin. "You gave me your card at the coffee shop."

He cleared his throat. "Is everything okay?"

"Not exactly."

"Okay," he drew out. "Are you calling to talk about something?"

Talk.

That was his specialty.

He won't like this.

"Not exactly. I need a ride."

The easiest solution to my problem would have been to hail a cab. I had done it countless times, but that wasn't happening, not in my state. Any decent cab driver would've either known who I was or driven me straight to the ER. That couldn't happen.

"You need to be more specific."

My shoulders sagged in relief. At least he was considering it. "I'm stranded."

"Stranded where?"

"An alley."

He mumbled out low-pitched words I couldn't make out.

"And I need a ride from said alley."

"An alley where?"

"In the city."

I gave him the directions.

Since I'd consumed all my energy escaping Oliver, I hadn't made it far from his place. I'd sprinted through his living room in a single heel like my name was Cinderella. Unfortunately, the man chasing me was no Prince Charming. Choosing to take the stairs over the elevator, I'd raced out of the building and bumped into the chilly night.

Did I think Oliver would hurt me? Yes.

Did I think he'd kill me? Probably not.

The dumbass didn't have the balls or the skills to dispose of my body and get away with it. He'd never risk his reputation or career for that.

"I'll be there in fifteen minutes," he said.

I heard movement in the background on his end.

"Get out of the alley and into the open, where you're visible."

"Okey dokey." I hesitated. Leaving the alley would put me into view of my predator.

"Screw it." I pushed away from the wall.

Oliver was too lazy to search for me. Asshole didn't like working for anything.

The icy wind assaulted me as I migrated onto the sidewalk, keeping my phone clutched to my ear. I stopped to give my body a rest after a few steps and leaned against a brick wall underneath an awning.

Rolling my eyes, I glanced down and observed tonight's outfit of choice—a short, strapless dress that hit the base of my thighs and open-toed heels. Well, *a heel* since I'd lost one.

As per usual, I'd chosen slutty over practical when Oliver picked me up from my place. I'd intended for my clothes to be off in minutes—which they were—and I'd be in his bed for the rest of the night. I hadn't foreseen being stranded in the middle of the night, freezing my ass off with a busted lip.

"Are you ready for this cock, baby?" Oliver asked, sliding his hand up and down his dick. His bloodshot eyes fixated on my bare breasts when I straddled his hips.

I licked my lips, stared down at him, and nodded.

"Now, fuck me," he rasped.

His mouth fell open when my hands replaced his, wrapping around his thickness and rubbing him against my wet folds.

"You're so wet for me," he said. "You're always so fucking wet when you see my dick."

I situated him in line with my opening and thrust myself down in one quick movement. He filled me completely, and I grinned wide when I felt his cock jerk against my walls.

I loved this power. I loved being in charge. He was bowing down to my pussy. That thrilled me.

Lust after me, asshole.

"Fuck yeah," he moaned, moving his hips.

I moaned, and my hands fell forward to level myself at the same time he snagged a nipple between his lips, sucking hard.

That feels good.

I gripped the sheets, riding him harder until I felt something— something that wasn't right—and that something pissed me off.

My head went blank as I clutched the cheap fabric in my hand. I stopped, but he continued to thrust underneath me, his eyes closed, clueless to what was impending.

"You asshole!" I screamed, slapping him across the face.

His eyes shot open. "Mmm, baby, you want to play it rough tonight? I like it." He rammed his hips up, grabbing my waist and slamming me down against him.

I held in a deep breath. The feeling of him inside of me was so good, but I had to stand my ground. I couldn't succumb to his dick when I was this angry.

I shoved the dirty panties in his mouth, and he coughed.

"What the hell?" he yelled, spitting them out.

My hand burned when it came into contact with his cheek again. "Whose are those?" I fumed.

He grunted when I pushed away from him and slid off the bed.

I grabbed my dress and pulled it over my head. "Fuck you, you stupid, cheating asshole."

He smacked his palm against the bed, his cock still hard, and groaned. "Elise, baby, it's not what it looks like. You're overreacting." He patted the space next to him. "Get back in bed. You know you want this dick."

"I don't want anything from you," I yelled, forcing myself to glance away before I caved. I snagged one of my heels from the floor while searching for the other.

He picked up the panties and held them above his face to examine them. "I'm pretty sure these are—"

"Don't you dare say they're mine," I cut him off. "I have an ass and don't wear cheap polyester G-strings. You could've at least cheated with a girl who wore decent panties."

He pulled himself up from the bed to grab his pants and slid them on. He didn't bother buckling them. He thought he was going to sweet-talk his way out of this. I didn't blame him. Oliver looked like a model, had a bank account like he worked on Wall Street, and had a dick like a porn star.

He rushed forward to stop me, capturing my elbow and squeezing it tightly.

"Take me home," I demanded.

He took a step forward.

I took a step back.

"Please, baby, just calm down and talk to me," he pleaded.

I shook my head, and when he pushed me back roughly, I fell against the wall.

"You're not leaving until you hear me out."

I tried to catch my breath. "We don't need to talk about anything. Take me home."

He crowded me. We were nose to nose, our mouths just inches apart, squaring each other up.

Nobody said no to a Hatfield. Oliver knew that. His family name *was as powerful as mine. Both of us were ready for the battle that was about to happen.*

Or, I stupidly thought, I was.

I could count the number of boyfriends I'd had with one hand.

If that's what you'd call them.

Every single one had been a cheating asshole. *Always.* It was inevitable. I blamed it on the type of men I dated and the fact that I wasn't intelligent enough to choose a different type. Random men you went home with from nightclubs or country club assholes your father had set you up with were never serious boyfriend material. I was practically asking to get cheated on.

And honestly, that relieved me. It was a get-out-of-jail-free card. When they cheated, it gave me a reason to dispose of them. We'd never last. We'd never fall in love, have some ridiculous, overpriced wedding, and drive a minivan, lugging our children around. We were using each other, momentarily getting what the other could provide, until someone better came along.

"Where are you?" Weston asked, startling me. "I'm pulling up to the corner."

I made out headlights approaching. "What are you driving?"

It wasn't a bright idea to go up to a random car on the corner, given that I looked like a two-bit, beaten-up hooker

"Black SUV. I'm flashing my lights."

"Got it."

I hopped on one foot in his direction. My ribs stabbed against my skin with each step. A car door slammed, and Weston joined me on the sidewalk.

"What the hell?" he screamed, peering at my feet. "Where is your shoe?"

I lost the weight of my body when he grabbed my arm, wrapping it around his shoulders, and he pulled me up from the ground. He kept me balanced against him while my feet hovered a few inches from the snow until we reached the car.

I shrugged. "I lost it."

He opened the car door, carefully kept his hold on me, and helped me into the heated leather seat. I situated myself as open vents blew warm air against my face.

"How did you lose your shoe in this weather?" he asked when he got in the car. "Why are you even wearing shoes like that?" He gestured out the window. "It's snowing."

Thank you, Captain Obvious.

"It's a long story," I answered.

The car went silent.

"That I don't want to tell."

He buckled his seat belt. "Fine. How about you explain what happened to your face then?"

"I don't want to talk about that either."

"I'm not pulling away from this spot until you do."

The interior light came on, burning my eyes and illuminating the inside of the car. Every bruise and cut on my face were in the spotlight. I had pain everywhere, but I wasn't sure exactly where each ache was coming from.

I'd taken a few blows to the face and had trouble opening one eye completely. Blood was on my swollen lips, and it felt like Oliver kicked me again every time I moved. I was positive my ribs were broken.

"Oh my God," he hissed, studying my face.

I flinched when his chilly fingers reached out, grabbed my chin, and examined me.

"We need to call the cops."

I smacked his hand away when he reached for his phone in the cupholder. "No cops."

His eyebrows crushed together. "What? We have to call the cops. I'll drive you to the station. You'll be safe with me. No one will hurt you again."

Too late for that.

"I'm not going to the cops."

My father would kick my ass if what had happened went public, and Oliver's family couldn't afford a scandal like this. His family had power over countless politicians, and my tattling would cost him all the pull he had in this city. Keeping my mouth shut was imperative.

"You were assaulted, and you're not going to report it?" Weston asked as if I'd lost my mind.

I nodded, completely aware I'd lost my mind long ago. "Correct."

"We at least need to call your dad. Maybe he'll talk some sense into you."

I would laugh if my face didn't hurt so badly.

"He's out of town," I lied.

There was no way in hell I was calling him. I would call Oliver's drunken, woman-beating ass before I dialed my father's number.

Weston clenched his jaw while eyeing me suspiciously. "I'm sure he has a cell phone, Elise."

"I'm not calling him," I snapped, losing patience.

"Then, we'll go to the hospital."

"We won't be going to the hospital either." My face would heal in a few days. I didn't need anyone else hearing about this.

He blew out a frustrated breath. "So, you don't want to go to the hospital, you don't want to go to the cops, and you don't want to tell me what happened?"

I nodded again. "That's right."

15

He scrubbed his hands over his clean-shaven face. "Then, why did you call me?"

I ignored the pain when I bit into the edge of my lip. "I didn't have anyone else to call."

His face fell. "Tell me what you'd like me to do for you. This goes against everything I stand for, but I can't force you to get help. Would you like me to take you home?"

I shook my head and sank back into my seat. "I can't go home like this."

I had a beaten-up face and was wearing a ripped dress and a single heel. There was no way my father wouldn't hear that I'd come walking through the entrance, resembling a battered hooker.

"Is there somewhere else I can take you?"

"I have nowhere else to go," I said in honesty.

If I went to the hospital, I'd be in trouble. If I went home and people saw me like this, there'd be repercussions.

"You can rent me a hotel room," I finally said, narrowing it down to my last resort. "It has to be a sketchy one, under your name, and you have to sneak me in. I have plenty of cash." I opened my clutch and pulled out a wad of hundred-dollar bills.

He shook his head. "That would look even worse. You can stay at my place, but this stays between us, okay? This could be bad for me."

"I'm good at keeping secrets." I shoved my money back into my bag.

He geared the car into drive but kept his foot on the break before pulling away. I grew nervous when his deep, dark eyes focused on me. Something was about to happen, and I felt I wouldn't like it.

"One more thing,"

I fidgeted with my seat belt. "What?"

16

"If I do this, you have to come to see me for therapy this week."

Is he crazy?

I shook my head and gave him my best one-eyed glare. "Nuh-uh, absolutely not. You can drop me back off at that corner because that's not happening." I wrapped my hand around the door handle, fully ready to make a run for it if necessary.

I shrieked at the sound of the car doors locking. "Did you just lock me in?" I asked, my face burning.

He held up three fingers. "Three meets. You agree to it, or I'm leaving the doors locked and calling the cops. Three meets. That's all I'm asking for. You agree, and I'll pull away right now."

He was blackmailing me. The asshole was blackmailing me.

"Fine. I'll play your ridiculous game."

"Promise me."

"What are we, in fifth grade? Would you like to circle pinkies and spit into each other's palm too?" I was throbbing everywhere. I didn't have the patience to deal with his psychological bullshit. "In case you haven't realized it, my head hurts, and I have blood all over me."

"Promise me—that's all you have to do. It's easy."

"Fine," I groaned out. "I promise."

three

ELISE

"Stay right there," Weston instructed, leveling me back against the wall of his apartment before shutting the door. He double-checked that I was stable before pulling away to turn on the lights.

Pain erupted through my body with every move I made. He'd thrown my shoe onto the floorboard of his car when we pulled into the parking garage and then carried me up the three flights of stairs that led to his apartment.

He tossed my clutch onto a marble countertop before coming back for me.

"Careful," he said, wrapping my trembling arm back around his shoulders.

He helped me to the couch in the middle of the living room. My bare thighs shivered as they grazed the leather when he attentively set me down.

"I'll be right back." He pulled away to walk into an open doorway, which gave me a chance to observe his place.

It wasn't decor expected from a guy his age. It was sophisticated. The furniture was tasteful and expensive. Books were stacked in the center of the black glass-top table with a shag rug beneath it. The brick fireplace had a large TV mounted above it, and two large abstract paintings were hung to each side. I blinked a few times, trying to make out the artist of the paintings with my one swollen eye but couldn't distinguish who it was.

He returned to the room with a cable-knit blanket in his arms. "Here." Bending down, he wrapped the blanket around my shivering body. "Let's get you cleaned up."

I gripped the blanket as he carefully pulled me up, and we took baby steps across the room. Each one—each excruciating step—was a reminder of what had happened to me.

We walked through a bedroom before landing in an adjoined bathroom. He eased me down on the closed toilet seat and began shuffling through drawers and cabinets. He grabbed a first aid kit and dropped on his knees in front of me. Capturing my chin in his hand, he examined my face.

"I bet you regret giving me your card." I forced a laugh—a lame attempt to kill the tension.

He didn't return the laugh. "This has to be killing you."

I flinched at the sting of peroxide when it met my broken skin.

"You need stitches. Are you sure you don't want to go to the hospital? It'll scar."

I grimaced at another sting. "No hospital."

He nodded, letting the subject go. I shut my eyes, relaxing at the feel of his hands carefully cleaning my wounds. He brushed a lukewarm washcloth over my puffy lips, erasing the blood around them, and then wiped off each finger.

"Whoever it was, they sure did a number on you," he said, double checking he hadn't missed anything. Resting his hands on my knees, he stared up at me. "How do your ribs feel?"

"Like they're cracking underneath my skin," I answered.

He lifted back up to his feet to wash his hands. "Do you want me to take a look?"

I gaped at him.

"To make sure they're not broken," he rushed out. "Which I'm positive they are, but if you don't feel comfortable, I understand."

"No, it's fine."

I'd been naked in front of plenty of men. He shouldn't be any different to me.

"You can leave your bra and panties on. Pull your dress up to your chest, and I'll get your sides wrapped up for you. Call for me when you're ready."

He handed me a towel and turned around to leave, but I stopped him.

I signaled to my dress. "I need help with this." There was no way I'd be able to get it off without his help. It was practically glued to my skin.

His face paled as he scratched his neck. "Okay ... can you raise your arms for me?"

They shook as I lifted them, and I held back the urge to scream out in pain. He fell to one knee, his face leveling with the apex of my thighs, and grabbed the hem of my dress.

My heart fluttered as a cold sweat broke out along my skin. My back stiffened, and I put all my attention on him. I scooted my hips forward. My pain started to suppress as I focused on something else. That something being how badly I suddenly wanted him to touch me.

I hung my head in shame when I felt the warmth building up between my legs. It was pathetic. I was getting turned on, growing wetter between my legs with each touch, while he was trying to take care of me. My imagination wandered to what would happen if he made a simple slip of the hand, allowing his fingers to roam between my thighs and venture into my pussy.

What the hell is wrong with me?

Weston was the opposite of my type. He was nice, sweet, nor seemed like he'd be a pick for this month's *Playgirl* magazine.

So, why was my body tingling in desperation for him? I was in awe at his attentiveness while he cleaned me up. He was a careful lover—I was sure of it. That was exactly what I didn't like. I wasn't a slow and sensual kind of girl. I liked it raw and unemotional. There were no emotions when a guy pulled my hair and slapped my ass while I rode him. We were just two people fucking to get our frustrations out. *So, why did I imagine how Weston was in bed?*

I parted my legs more, giving him a silent invitation I hoped he'd pick up, but he ignored my coaxing. His long fingers latched on to the hem of my dress, bunching up the fabric in his hand. He moved in closer, his breathing picking up, and he started dragging it up my body. He stopped when it hit underneath my ass.

"Lift up for me," he said, grabbing my hip to assist me.

I whimpered, watching his jaw drop and his pupils dilate when he noticed I wasn't wearing any panties.

He coughed while shaking his head. "I'm not going to ask."

He attempted to slide the dress up my chest, but his hands abruptly stopped when I cried out in agony. He waited for directions on what to do next.

"Cut it," I demanded.

"What?"

"Cut this damn thing off."

It was an eight-hundred-dollar dress, but it was already ruined. He pulled himself up to grab a pair of scissors from the kit and hooked the handle of the scissors between his fingers.

Anxiousness riddled through me, as I wanted his hands to touch me again.

Did he feel the same way?

Did he want me as bad as I wanted him?

Maybe we'd end up in his bed, and he'd take care of me in a more entertaining way.

He stepped forward, the scissors hitting the fabric as he held up my dress and began cutting. He didn't venture between my thighs or cleavage. The dress split in two, skimming the pit between my breasts, and he did a double take when he noticed I wasn't wearing a bra. I wasn't a fan of undergarments. The dress fell off my body.

He grabbed the bandage from the floor and began wrapping my sides. "I'll try to be as careful as I can. I'm leaving it a little loose, so we don't damage your lungs."

The pain died down with each wrap. He finished, grabbed the blanket, and wrapped it back around my body.

"I have a guest room and bath down the hall. You probably want to shower and clean yourself up. Try not to get the bandage too wet," he said.

My stomach twisted in disappointment. Sadly, it seemed sharing his bed wasn't in the plans tonight.

"Yeah, I'll be fine," I replied.

He helped me to the guest bathroom and handed me a towel. "Keep the door unlocked and yell for me if you need anything."

I unraveled the blanket when he left and leaned against the vanity as I waited for the water to warm. I shoved my hand through my hair and stared closely at my reflection.

I could make out the faint bruises along my cheeks. One of my eyes was swollen shut. My lip was busted, my hair a ratted mess. I spread my fingers along the scratches on my neck and saw more along my breasts.

He was right. Oliver had done a number on me.

I carefully climbed into the shower, my sore skin burning as the water ran down it. I rested my hand against the wall to balance myself, letting the water stream down my body as I cried.

After my shower, I walked into the bedroom and found a pair of sweats and a T-shirt. I headed back into the living room after changing.

"Are you hungry?" Weston asked, standing in the kitchen. "I can make you a sandwich or some soup, if you'd like?"

I yawned. "I'm going to go to bed. I'm exhausted."

He turned around to grab a glass of water and ibuprofen. He dropped a few pills in his hand and held them out for me. "You'll need these to make it through the night. Let me know if there's anything else I can help with. Good night, Elise."

I noticed my phone and clutch sitting on the nightstand when I walked back into the room. I slid into the cold sheets, inhaling the scent of fresh cotton, and knew I'd be fighting sleep.

Not many people had ever helped me like Weston. Bella, my nanny growing up, helped me, but she received a paycheck for it. But Weston wasn't getting anything in return, and he treated me better than anyone.

four

WESTON

I'd been a fixer for as long as I could remember. I had been the person my brother and sister came to with their problems. I'd helped my parents keep my brother out of trouble. I fixed my elderly neighbor's pipes when they got clogged and helped her carry up groceries every Sunday morning.

If there was a problem, I fixed it. I didn't like people to be broken.

"I'm so screwed," I muttered, watching Elise disappear into my guest room.

I shouldn't have let her come here. I was an idiot. Her being here could cost me everything I'd worked my ass off for.

This reckless woman could ruin my entire career.

I needed her gone, and I needed to find the fortitude to make it happen. For some reason, I couldn't muster up the power to tell her to get out. My mind was disoriented, messing with my decisions. As bad as it was, I liked her here.

I blew out a breath as I went back to my bathroom to clean up. My gaze shot directly to the ripped-up dress thrown in the corner. My throat burned as I scooped it up, skating my fingertips along the satin that smelled of flowery perfume.

I rubbed the back of my neck, using my knuckles to knead into my tense skin. I'd had my hands on her. I'd seen plenty of naked women in my life, but even with cuts and bruises, she was the most breathtaking.

My brain swept back to what I'd tried to ignore. My touch had turned her on. I could tell. I'd ached, wanting to cave into my desire, but I held back. I couldn't do that. I wasn't that kind of guy. She didn't need me hitting on her in a moment of weakness. A man had beaten her up. She sure hadn't needed another groping her a few hours later.

My chest constricted, anger boiling inside me, when I noticed the dark red blood splatters smeared against the black fabric. I knotted the dress up, my pulse shoving into my throat, and snatched the scissors. I rammed the blades through it, not stopping until the material lay in tiny slivers at my feet.

I didn't know who had hurt her, but I was certain it'd been a man. I despised men who put their hands on women. Scratch that. They couldn't even be classified as men. They were pussies, and she needed to quit hanging out with pussies. Real men respected women, loved women, and they sure didn't beat them to a bloody pulp and then leave them stranded in an alley.

I tossed the remnants of the dress into the trash can on my way back to my bedroom and collapsed onto my bed without bothering to undress.

I wanted to scream at her and insist she quit making such stupid decisions.

For some reason, Elise fascinated me. Maybe because I'd never met anyone like her before. She self-destructed like it was her middle name, inflicting herself with as much pain as possible. I didn't understand her, but I wanted to.

I should've turned around and ran when I spotted her at the

coffee shop. I waited in line, using every ounce of self-control to not stare at her. Even with the few glances I managed to sneak in, there was no mistaking it was her.

The woman sitting only a few feet away had been selfish and insecure. Her brown eyes, which had once stared at me with such hate, were burned into my brain. The color reminded me of the autumn leaves that fell yearly at my grandfather's property in Tennessee.

Her glossy jet-black hair was swept back in a loose braid that fell to the crook of her neck—the same style she'd worn three years ago. Her cherry-red lips parted each time she took a long drink from her cup.

It was humiliating to admit, but I'd dreamed about her. Not so frequently anymore, but I did almost nightly after we met. I'd shut my eyes at night, my mind wandering back to the girl who'd perplexed me on my very first day. I'd been inexperienced and didn't know how to handle her.

I stood there, repeatedly telling myself to grab my coffee and get out of there. I told myself not to go there, but I didn't stick with my plan. Instead, I grabbed my coffee and headed directly to her. I was helplessly pulled in her direction, losing all control over my body.

I had so many questions for her. I wanted to know the rest of her story. I wanted to know why she was here in Chicago. I wanted her to let me in, like I'd begged her to years ago.

But she acted like she couldn't even stand to look at me. Her lips had grimaced like my presence made her uncomfortable, so I'd left my business card and walked away, doubting she'd ever use it.

Giving her that card was the stupidest yet smartest decision I'd ever made. If she hadn't had my number, I would've never been able to rescue her.

I wanted to know what had happened to her tonight. I wanted to know who'd hurt her and how bad the damage was. Then, I wanted to fix every piece of her.

five

WESTON

THREE YEARS EARLIER

I was twenty-five, newly graduated from earning my doctorate in psychology, and had just completed my internship. The market was saturated and finding a job had been hell. Sun Gate Rehabilitation Center was five hours away from Chicago, but they were willing to hire a new guy, and the pay was decent. Not great, but decent. So, I'd packed up my things and left the Windy City for the Indiana cornfields.

I met her on my first day. My first two patient appointments had gone through smoothly, and I was building up some confidence. Then, she showed up with her attitude and sharp nails and deflated it.

I hadn't been ready for Elise. I hadn't been prepared for this sassy fireball to come barreling in and shoot me flames of attitude as her defense mechanism. She was trying to shield herself because she didn't want me to see the pain and hate exploding through her.

My superiors had given me her backstory. Elise was a spoiled seventeen-year-old girl on a mission to destroy herself and didn't care who or what she took down with her. She misbehaved when things didn't go her way, spending her free time drinking in nightclubs and experimenting with drugs. She was caught screwing one of her father's business partners and a few other older men. She had done all that to get back at her father because he was so protective of her.

Even with all that forewarning, I still hadn't been ready. There was no preparation for this woman flying down the hallway with full force, her face twisted with fury as she glared at me standing in the doorway. She looked like she wanted to rip my head off and stomp on it before I even said a word to her.

My job was about to get challenging.

"I'm surprised they sent you," she said, stopping in front of me and narrowing her eyes.

"Why's that?" I asked.

"They usually don't send men because I fuck them."

What the hell?

"I can assure you, that won't happen." My chest locked up, a giant lump lodging itself in the pit of my throat.

She smiled wickedly. "You sure about that?"

I gulped down the lump. I wasn't sure if she had told me that for shock value or if she was being honest. Those above me had told me she liked to play mind games. There was no way they'd hide that she'd been intimate with other psychologists.

"So ... who the fuck are you?" she asked, her hands flying to her hips.

I took a moment to stare at the girl who'd been labeled *unstable* and *out of control*. She was breathtakingly gorgeous. I felt like a complete jackass for thinking that because she was only seventeen, but there was no denying it.

It wasn't an *I want to sleep with you* kind of beauty. Her features—from the long, dark hair in a braid to the plump lips and the endless curves—were attractive. Those brown eyes of hers leveled on me as if I were her prey for the day.

She might've been pretty on the outside, but she was hideous, dark, and deceptive on the inside.

"I'm Dr. Weston Snyder," I said calmly. "I'm your doctor for the remainder of your stay."

I grunted when she squeezed her way into the room, her hip pushing into my stomach, and my side collided with the doorframe.

"Where the hell is Patterson?" she snapped when she noticed the room was empty.

I shut the door behind us. "She resigned. I'm taking over her patients."

They had fired Patterson because she let her patients watch Netflix instead of helping them with their problems. I was positive this girl had taken full advantage of that too. That sure wasn't happening with me.

She fell on the couch as I shuffled around the room, gathering my things. I snatched up a folder from the edge of the desk and rolled a chair forward until we were sitting only a few inches apart.

I took in a deep breath of courage. *This is a teenage girl. Why is she intimidating me?* I needed to get it together. I'd gone through years of school and training to deal with people like her.

"I've studied your file," I began, opening the folder in my lap. I scratched my head and focused on the first page. "Why don't we go over your history? Get to know each other? We can talk about why you're here."

That's a good start. I was doing what I'd been trained to do in school. *Let them talk to you. Allow them to open up. Gain their trust.*

I waited for her to reply, but she sat quietly playing with her braid.

Well, that plan will not work.

I crossed my legs and took a deep breath to calm my nerves. "Let's start with your drug and alcohol addiction history."

That got a reaction out of her.

She snorted and pushed a few loose strands of hair away from her face. "Drug addiction? No."

I leaned back in my chair and opened my mouth to argue, but slammed it shut when she kept talking.

"Yes, I drink and take pills *recreationally*, but I don't have an addiction."

"Those pills are narcotics," I pointed out. "Narcotics are drugs."

"Look, *Weston*, it's not like I'm shooting heroin into my veins or hanging out in some beat-up garage in a sketchy neighborhood, smoking meth."

"I see you're still in denial," I said, settling my gaze on her. "You've overdosed twice. I'm sorry, Miss Parks, deny it all you want, but you have an addiction."

She held up a finger. "First off, don't call me Miss Parks. My name is Elise." She curled her upper lip. "And recheck your facts, *Doctor*. Those overdoses were over two years ago. I know my limits now. You try living in my hell. Tell me you wouldn't be doing anything to numb yourself too."

"You shouldn't have limits because you shouldn't be doing these things."

She waved her hand in the air, and her tone turned nasty as she changed the subject. "What else do you allegedly know about me?"

Apparently, she was calling the shots.

I peered down at the paper. "Sexual promiscuity, preferably with older men."

She flinched, every muscle in her body tensing up, and paled. The room suddenly shifted.

That's it.

Her trigger.

What she's most afraid of.

She regained her composure and shot me an annoyed glare. "I will not deny that I have sex, probably more than I should, but it happens. But as far as the other part, the jab in my spine to keep me down, I think it's unfair to classify it as promiscuity."

"Why is that?"

Her guard was coming down, and I couldn't wait to dig in. I wanted to crack open her mind and discover everything hidden inside.

"Does being held down, my legs pried open, while someone shoves themself inside me mean I'm promiscuous?"

I almost fell out of my chair. My mind spun as I scrambled for the right words.

What? Why didn't anyone tell me?

"Are you telling me you were raped?" I asked, hastily flipping through the pages. "There's no mention of you being sexually assaulted in here." I kept turning pages, skimming over words.

Then, I found them—two small, almost-hidden words.

Peter Kline.

"Are you talking about Peter Kline?" I asked, tapping my finger against the name.

She threw her head back and groaned. "No, I'm not talking about Peter Kline. I fucked him willingly. I'm so sick of him being used as a cop-out. I'm talking about the other guys."

"I'm sorry, but I'm not seeing more," I said slowly. "Have you told anyone else?"

"Of course, I have, jackass. Are you calling me a liar?"

I shook my head. "I'm not calling you a liar," I stammered.

I needed to investigate this. *Why would other psychologists have left this out?*

Her eyes brightened as a slow smile built along her lips. "So, you believe me then?"

"I don't know enough facts to answer that, but if you're telling me that's what happened, then I believe you."

They told me she was deceptive, but would she lie about being raped?

"Then, tell someone."

She didn't feed me any more details. She got up and walked out the door while I stayed frozen in my seat, asking myself had just happened.

I tried my best to focus on other patients the rest of my day, but I couldn't get her out of my head. After my last session, I went to Sun Gate's director to tell him what she'd told me.

That was when I found out Elise Parks was a liar.

She had problems that I wasn't equipped to handle yet. I could deal with addicts. I could help self-harmers, but I couldn't manage a manipulative teen trying to puzzle my mind.

And I couldn't afford to lose my job or get sued.

six

ELISE

I groaned, feeling every muscle of my body convulse in pain, and opened an eye. I rested my head back comfortably against the pillow and stared in confusion at the white ceiling.

Who does this ceiling belong to?

It wasn't mine.

It wasn't Oliver's.

My stomach fluttered.

Shit. I'd broken one of my rules and stayed overnight with a random hookup.

The space was empty when I reached across the bed to feel for another warm body. I grew dizzy, racking my brain to remember last night's events.

I stilled at the sound of movement and held in a breath before turning to see who it was. The night came back in flashes.

I shut my eyes.

I'm still asleep. Get out of here. Go back to your bedroom and let me sneak out.

"Good morning."

I squeezed my eyes shut tighter at his cheerful voice. *Who's that happy in the morning?*

"Nice try," he said around a laugh. "I know you're awake, so quit faking it. I brought food."

"I'm not hungry," I grumbled.

"Too bad. You need to eat something. Your body needs replenishment if you want it to heal."

"My body needs replenishment?" I mocked, opening my eyes. "I'm fully capable of feeding myself."

He ignored me, and I glared at him when a tray of food was dropped onto my lap.

"Eggs and toast," he said.

I carefully brought myself up to rest my back against the bed's headboard. My stomach growled when I eyeballed the tray. Scrambled eggs. Toast with jelly. Fruit. Orange Juice. Two ibuprofens.

"Thanks," I half-whispered, my voice sounding scratchy against my sore throat. I grabbed the toast and took a small bite. "Why are you doing this? Why did you help me, and why are you being so nice?"

He sat on the bed, wearing a Columbia University T-shirt and sweatpants. "You were alone in the city, beaten up, and needed help. I'm glad you called." His dark eyes set on mine like he was trying to remind me of everything that had happened.

I nodded and shoved a forkful of eggs into my mouth.

He ran his hands through his shaggy, morning-messy hair. "I'm almost certain you know who did this to you." He continued to lecture, his voice sincere. "I hope you end whatever relationship you have with him. You deserve more than being beaten up and left in some dirty alley. But you'll never get that if you don't believe in yourself, Elise."

seven

ELISE

"Are you planning on dragging your ass out of bed today?" the ear-piercing voice shouted while my bedroom door flew open.

I kept my eyes shut but could sense his footsteps growing closer. I hated that he had a key to my apartment.

"Let me guess. You've been out all night, partying again?" He scoffed. "Typical."

I opened my eyes to find my father standing beside my bed. I shoved my face deeper into my silk pillowcase, ignoring the ache penetrating through my face.

"It's two in the afternoon, Elise," he continued to scold when he realized I wasn't planning on answering him.

I yawned loudly but stayed quiet. It was the best way to deal with him. *Keep your mouth shut because they will use anything you say or do against you.*

"Fucking answer me!" he ordered.

I held back the urge to scream when the chill of the room smacked into me as he pulled my blanket off, exposing me. I

36

still didn't lift my head. I was a professional at playing his games.

Let me freeze. Let him see my half-naked body. I didn't care.

"Answer me!"

Screw it. I'll let him win today.

"I was taking a nap, okay? I feel like crap," I finally answered.

I was beaten up, sore as hell, and my brain played kickball with my skull. The past twelve hours had consisted of me refraining from moving as much as possible to save my body from suffering any more distress than it had to.

"Get up, get dressed, and meet me in the living room," he demanded. "And put on some goddamn clothes."

I was wearing Weston's sweatshirt and a pair of boy shorts. "I'm sleeping in my bed *alone*, in my apartment, where I live *alone*. I usually don't do that in full ball gowns."

He snorted. "I'm sure that's something new for you, waking up alone."

"Oh, screw you!" I snatched my comforter and covered myself back up.

"Meet me in the living room," he said, shaking his head and leaving my bedroom. "And don't take your sweet little time. I know how you are."

"Asshole," I muttered.

Weston had dropped me off at the back entrance early this morning, and I snuck in, wearing his clothes. I'd gone from resembling a hooker to looking homeless in less than twelve hours. As soon as I got home, I stripped down, unwrapped my ribs, and took another shower to rid myself of any excess Oliver grime. Then, I'd put Weston's sweatshirt back on, snuggled into my bed, and let his calming scent put me to sleep.

My muscles strained against my skin when I pulled myself

up and grabbed a pair of pajama shorts. I tried to hide my limp while making my way into the living room.

"Nosy much?" I snapped when I found him rifling through my clutch.

He dumped the contents on my kitchen table, examining each item to find something incriminating. "Care to explain why your face is busted in?" he asked, dropping my bag in failure.

I shrugged. "It's nothing."

"Nothing, my ass," he growled, stomping toward me. With each stride, his face contorted with more hate and disgust. "Don't you dare lie to me." He stood in front of me, rapidly breathing as he stared down with repulsion.

Clint Parks was a very wealthy man, and with wealth came power. He was also malicious, controlling, and hungry to keep that power in his grip.

I hated this man.

He hated me.

"Explain yourself," he demanded.

He was in his late fifties, and there was no denying he was attractive for his age. The dark color of his hair matched mine apart from a few salt-and-pepper grains sprinkled throughout the strands. His chest was broad and authoritative. His stature was intimidating, the evil smirk on his face threatening, and the millions of dollars in his bank account only added to his power. He was a businessman, owning several high-end hotels in the heart of Chicago, a few investment companies, and practically the entire Gold Coast Historic District, where we lived.

"I slipped in the shower and hurt myself." I was never one to be quick on my toes.

When his hand forcefully curled around my upper arm, I whimpered, holding in a cry.

"I know what happened to your pretty little face. I was

simply inquisitive to see if you'd tell me the truth or not, which you didn't." He shook his head. "That's not surprising."

"You want the truth?" I asked, my bare feet pushing into the soft, plush carpet. "Fine, here's the truth for you. Oliver did this." I pointed to my face. "He's the one who busted my face by punching it. He also kneed me in the ribs, pulled my hair, and headbutted me!"

His nostrils flared as he prepared to spit his fire. "When are you going to quit with the lies?"

"You don't even know what happened. So, don't you dare say I'm lying."

His hand added pressure to my skin as he took a step closer, and I didn't dare take a step back. "Oh, I know exactly what happened. Oliver called this morning. He said you flew off the handle, attacking him because he'd found pills in your bag and confronted you about sleeping with someone else. When he asked about your cheating, you got pissed and left with some guy who picked you up from his place. I'm sure whatever slime-ball you're seeing behind his back is the one who beat you."

I wanted to kill Oliver. I wanted to twist his dick so hard that the blood flow stopped and it fell limp in front of his thousand-dollar shoes.

Jackass.

"Do you seriously believe that lie?" I asked in disbelief, throwing my arm out to gesture to myself. "He did this."

"You're a lunatic, drug addict, and a whore."

"I didn't have anything in my purse. You drug-test me twice a week, every week, so you know I'm clean."

I pulled away, sneaking around him before he had the chance to stop me. I headed into the kitchen for a glass of water and searched for something for my pain, hoping he wouldn't follow me. But I'd never been one to have my hopes fulfilled.

"When is this bullshit going to stop?" he asked, crowding

around me. He leveled his eyes on me, getting closer into my space.

I stumbled backward. *Shoot.* I shouldn't have let him corner me. I was like one of those idiots in the horror movies who ran through the deserted cornfield instead of jumping in the getaway car a few feet away.

"Why can't you ever be honest?" His voice was strangled. "Why do you have to be like your whore mother? You like to flaunt it. Oh, yes, you love to flaunt it with this long, dark hair." His hand raised, his fingers grazing my hair, causing me to shiver. "Those curves that developed way too young."

I froze when his hand dropped from my head to roam down my side, giving me goose bumps.

"But you can't deal with the repercussions of your whoring ways. You keep acting like a slut, spreading your legs to every man, you're going to get beaten up a few times, baby girl."

I looked away from him, my hands itching to shove him back, but I was smarter than that. "Why would I hit him first? That doesn't even make sense," I croaked out.

I let out a rush of relief when his hand left my side and his arms settled to each side of me on the counter, caging me in.

"Oliver is an intelligent and responsible man," he said. "He wouldn't make up a ridiculous story like that."

"But I would?"

His face was so close that he practically spat on me with every word. "You can. It's flowing through half your blood. It's what you do. You enjoy playing the victim. You want the attention. It turns you on and eats you alive when you don't receive it."

"You're just like Oliver. Maybe that's why Mom couldn't stand you. That's why she hated your guts."

I inserted that verbal knife, twisted it into the small sliver of a heart he had, and relished in his hurt, like he did mine. Like father, like daughter. You couldn't escape or destroy the monster without becoming one yourself.

I cried out when my head rammed back into the cabinet, his rough palm connecting with my already-sore cheek. "Don't you dare talk about your bitch mother. She didn't deserve a man like me. She was nothing but a poor cunt I took off the streets."

He hated her, but he was still in love with her.

He'd take his love for her to the grave.

His finger poked in front of my face. "This is my last warning. Stop with the antics, the fits, and your erratic behavior, or your apartment will be gone, and you'll be back to living with me. I might not be able to admit you anymore, but I will always control you. Remember that."

He pushed off the counter, stalked out of the kitchen, and left without saying another word. He'd said what he needed to say. He'd gotten his point across and didn't care what I had to say about it. He always had to have the last word.

I sagged down the cabinet, landing on the chilly tiles, but didn't cry. I sat there, staring blankly at the floor, and didn't move.

I'd had too many bad things hit me to cry over something that small. When bad things repeatedly happen to you, you learned to hold everything in. There was no crying—only numbness. You surrendered your emotions because you'd already given everything you had. Emptiness was all you had left.

I knew what people said about me. I knew I got mocked.

Poor little rich girl is upset her daddy yelled at her.

That wasn't the case. Those people had no clue what I'd gone through. They had no clue what that man had done to me.

An hour passed before I pulled myself up from the floor and went to the freezer. I grabbed a tub of ice cream and held it to my cheek.

"Asshole," I muttered, filling a glass with water and carrying my ice cream to the living room.

I had gotten my place last year and loved it even if it was directly across the hall from my father. It wasn't freedom to some people, but it was to me. I'd never had a place of my own. I'd been allowed to choose my furniture, and I'd gone eccentric. My couch was bright purple with white furry pillows scattered across it.

I flipped on the TV and turned on a rerun of *Sex and the City* before opening the ice cream and shoving a bite of mint chocolate chip into my mouth. I paused the TV when my phone rang and scowled at the screen, debating on answering.

"Hey," I answered, picking up on the fourth ring.

"How are you feeling?" Weston asked.

"All right. I took some medicine to help with the pain. I just need to pull out my high-coverage makeup." I lifted my legs and rested them on the coffee table.

"You can still go to the police. I'll go with you."

I rolled my eyes. He was delusional if he thought that was an option. I'd only become more of a mockery.

"No, I can't," I replied.

He sighed. "Don't forget what you promised me."

"I don't remember promising anything," I lied, shoving another bite into my mouth.

"You said you would."

"Oh, no, buddy, not happening. I hate therapy, and I'm old enough not to be forced into it anymore."

"I'm not asking you to do therapy. I'm asking you to talk to me."

I huffed. "Same difference."

"I did what you asked me to do," he said, growing aggravated. "Are you going to go back on your word?"

I should've called him private last night, so he couldn't bug me about that. "You know if my father finds out, he will not be happy about it."

Obviously, I'd quit seeing Weston for a reason. There was no way I could go there without my father knowing. He had eyes and ears everywhere.

"He won't find out. I'll meet you at my friend's office. We'll talk there. I'm texting you the address now."

Damn, he already had a plan and everything.

"Fine, I'll be there."

Fuck me.

eight

ELISE

I tossed lavender oil and Epsom salts into my bath as soft music flowed through my bathroom. Candlelight flickered around me as I sank into the hot water.

I'd tried to drown myself once. I was fourteen, and it was on the eve of what my father referred to as *the day she died*. I held my breath before ducking my head underneath the calm water, and after only a few seconds, my lips opened. The water seeped into my mouth, filling my lungs, while my nose fought for air. But I couldn't take it.

Before everything went black, before my life was officially over, my head flew up. Water dripped down my face while I took deep, heavy breaths and mentally screamed at myself for being such a coward. I didn't have the guts to go through with it. I needed someone else to do the job. I needed that starting push in front of the train. I needed someone to hold the pillow to my face and refuse to let go. I thought pills would do the job for me, but they failed me every time.

So, on my eighteenth birthday, I decided I was done. I obviously didn't want to die bad enough if I kept failing. My mind switched from being a victim to being a survivor. I wouldn't allow anyone else to win by taking myself out. I was going to live, to make myself happy, and let all those sick, sadistic bastards know they couldn't bring me down. I'd decided to find my inner bitch, my inner fighter, and run with her.

I jerked up at the sound of someone calling my name.

"I'm in the bathtub," I yelled, tilting my head back to relax. "I'll get out and meet you in the living room."

I shrieked when the door flew open and my father stalked in. I instantly lowered one hand underneath the water, using it to cover between my legs, and draped an arm across my breasts.

"Do you mind?" I snapped, glaring at him.

He'd never understood the concept of boundaries.

"Shut the hell up, Elise," he yelled, glaring at me. His eyes didn't linger, but he didn't glance away either. "I came to tell you I'm going to be out of town for the next few days. I asked Marlon to stay behind if you need a ride anywhere. Try to stay out of trouble."

Thank God. He wouldn't know about my trip to see Weston tomorrow. I'd dodge Marlon and take a cab.

I rolled my eyes, my hands shivering under the water. "I won't go out and do anything stupid. You know that, so why don't you quit repeating the same speech every day? Get over it and move the hell on. I have."

His nose turned up, his upper lip curling, and he took a whiff of the scent drifting through the room. "Your mom used to burn those candles."

I smiled at the mention of her. "I like them."

Lavender vanilla. It was my favorite scent. Bella had bought me a candle a few years ago and told me the same thing. So, I'd stocked up on them and burned them every night.

"They fucking reek. Get rid of them," he said in disgust.

I had to get rid of anything that reminded him of her. He'd taken every picture, every memory, everything, so I couldn't remember her. He didn't want to relive the memories. He couldn't be reminded of the woman who'd left him. He hated her. He despised her more than anyone. And he hated my resemblance to her.

nine

ELISE

"I've missed you, girl," Holly screeched, walking in front of me in eight-inch heels with a drink in each hand.

The brooding bouncer moved the rope to the side, letting us into the VIP area. Even though we were underage, all we had to do was hand over a few hundred-dollar bills, show a little cleavage, and we'd get a private table.

I used to be jealous of Holly when we were growing up. I'd wanted her looks. She reminded me of a Barbie doll. She was tall, almost six-two, skinny, and her hair was a natural blonde that people paid hundreds of dollars to achieve.

I wanted her family. They weren't dysfunctional. Her parents were still together and spent their free time traveling the world. Her mom took her shopping. They got manicures and had girls' trips. She had the mother-daughter relationship I'd always wished for.

But I'd been growing apart from Holly the past few months. I realized my life was less chaotic when we weren't together.

Not that I didn't love her. She'd been there for me through my hardest times, my sidekick during my drunken binges, and we'd even shared a jail cell a time or two.

I grabbed a drink from her hand and took a gulp. "Maybe if you got out of your boyfriend's ass, you'd see me more," I said with a fixed stare.

I wasn't trying to be a bitch, but she'd been ditching me for him more and more lately, and then she'd try to act like it was my fault.

She waved her hand through the air, her bright pink lips sucking on her straw. "You know how new relationships are." She fell on the couch, and I did the same next to her. "Plus, we made a pact to do the best-friend thing. I was supposed to date Quinton, you were supposed to date Oliver, and we'd hang out all the time."

"Yeah, that plan went to hell when Oliver decided to use me as a personal punching bag."

"He was drunk, Elise." She forced a laugh. "You have to admit, we've done some pretty stupid things while drunk."

"Sure, we have, but it never included causing bodily harm to someone."

She flipped her long hair over her shoulder. "He made a mistake. Give him another chance. He feels bad about it."

"Hell no," I snapped, standing up from the couch and gesturing to the sea of blurry bodies gyrating on the dance floor. "There are plenty of men out there. I don't need to settle for some woman-abusing asshole."

"But why not, baby?"

I whipped around at the sound of his cocky voice.

"Seriously, Holly?" I shouted, signaling to Oliver and Quinton standing across from me. "You invited them?"

"I thought you two could talk it out," she said, sauntering over to kiss Quinton on the lips.

"This was supposed to be a girls' night."

"I know," she whined. "I told Quinton that."

Quinton, wearing a suit, wrapped his arms around Holly's waist, dipping his hands down to grab handfuls of her ass. "We thought you ladies might like the surprise. Plus, I didn't want any assholes trying to get with my girl."

I rolled my eyes at him in disgust.

"Elise, baby, come on," Oliver begged, taking a step toward me and spreading his arms out. "I made a mistake. You were drinking. I was messed up. Things got out of hand."

"Listen," Quinton said, releasing Holly and walking between the two of us. He stared at me. "Quit acting like you have morals, Elise. You know you miss his cock, so hike your pretty little dress up and give him what you both use each other for." He threw his hands out toward Oliver. "You know he was on X, and anything goes when you're that fucked up. You're in a completely different zone."

My eyes swung back to Oliver. "You were on ecstasy?"

He shrugged shamelessly. "Yeah, I popped one before you came over. I didn't tell you because I knew you'd freak out, like you are now. You've been acting like a prude lately, but you know how much better sex feels when you're tripping.'"

Holly came to my side and slapped my arm. "Elise, I agree on the bore thing. Lighten up." She held out a pill in front of me, stuck it onto her tongue, and washed it down with her vodka and cranberry. "And you know I have an extra for you." She pulled out another and held it out to me.

I shook my head. "I told you, I can't do that anymore. My father has been drug-testing me nonstop."

"Since when has that ever stopped you?"

"Since he threatened to take away my apartment."

"Move in with me," Oliver suggested, moving in closer.

"Stay away from me," I said, holding my drink out to stop

him from coming any further. "I can't believe you think we'd get back together, let alone that I'd move in with you."

"What the fuck?" he asked defensively. "It's not like I did any damage. You still look pretty good, baby."

"I look good because I packed makeup on my face and I'm not moving around." I held back the urge to throw my drink in his face and kick him down like he had me.

"You're really not going to forgive me? Are you kidding me?" He straightened the collar on his shirt, his lips twisting into an angry scowl.

I took a long pull from the straw in my glass. "No, I'm really not."

Holly fell onto Quinton's lap on the couch. "Quit being a snob, Elise. What happened to my best friend?"

"I'm not being a snob. I don't want to be around him, and as my best friend, you should understand that," I argued, my voice turning cold.

"Fine, fuck you, bitch," Oliver said, letting out a bitter laugh. He grabbed a woman passing by around the waist and brought her into his chest. "You think you're the only willing pussy around this place?" He nodded his head Quinton's way. "Call me later, man."

I grabbed a shot glass on the table and drained its contents before throwing it at him. "Go fuck yourself."

The girl giggled when he grabbed her ass and pulled her against his crotch. "Oh, baby, I plan on having her do that for me tonight."

I turned my back on him, ignoring the insults flinging from his mouth, and crashed down onto the opposite end of the couch. I casted a glance to Holly to find her making out with Quinton.

Quinton's eyes twinkled in interest when he noticed me

staring and pulled away from her. "How about you join us?" he asked, running his hand along his chin. "Tell me how I compare to my friend."

I took another shot, flipped him off, and stormed away. I needed to find a new group of friends.

ten

ELISE

Weston: Good morning! Don't forget about me today. I'll have doughnuts as bribery.

I read his text and shook my head.

He was relentless.

I threw my phone down onto the bathroom counter, dried my hair, and stared at my face in the mirror. I trailed the tips of my fingers along my bare cheek. The bruises were fading, and my busted lip was healing. I hoped my ribs would play catch-up soon.

———

"Let me call you back," the teenage girl half-whispered into her cell when she noticed me walk in. She giggled before hanging up and moving her attention to me.

I'd dodged Marlon, snuck out, and hailed a cab to the

address Weston had given me. I gave the driver the address, shoved a pair of Chanel sunglasses over my hungover eyes, and stared out the window until we reached a charming, bright yellow residential house that had been converted into an office building. A sign held up by two chains and a wooden post had let me know I was entering the office of Dr. Wendy Milkins.

"Hi," the girl chirped. "Do you have an appointment?"

"No. I'm looking for Weston," I answered, not quite sure how to explain my reasoning for being there. I searched the room for him.

She pushed her sparkly blue fingernails through her bleached-blonde curls before picking up the phone. "Hey," she said into the speaker. "That girl is here."

That girl? What did she mean by that girl?

She nodded a few times, chewing on a pen, and hung up. I waited for her instructions on where to go, but she just creepily stared.

"I see my doughnut bribe worked."

I turned to find Weston standing tall in a doorway with a doughnut in his hand.

His curls were swept back into a baseball cap, and he appeared casual in a sweatshirt and jeans. "Doughnuts always work magic," he added, grinning, clearly pleased with himself that I'd shown up.

I kicked my leg out to the side and glared at him. "No, it was more along the lines of your irritating determination. I knew you wouldn't let it go until I came here and shut this down."

"Follow me," he said with a chuckle, jerking his head toward the room behind him.

I huffed, following his instructions, and walked into an office. He stayed on my heels, shut the door, and pointed to a black sofa in the middle of the room.

The office was typical. I'd been to plenty of psychologist

offices, and this one was just as generic as the others. A couch was in the middle with a box of tissues conveniently sitting on a table next to it. Self-help books that'd never be read lined the walls, and a doctorate degree hung high with pride behind the desk.

"Take off your sunglasses," he demanded.

"I have a headache," I grumbled, moving away from him to sit down.

"You're not going to sit here this entire time with sunglasses covering your eyes."

I snarled and dragged the glasses off my face. "You happy?" I squinted a few times, allowing my eyes to adjust to the excruciatingly bright room.

"I know you're not hungover."

"I made it here, didn't I? Don't judge me."

He walked toward the front of the room, shaking his head. "I'm sorry, but did you forget you were just beaten up the other night? Don't you think you need to make better choices?"

"I went out with a girlfriend," I replied in annoyance. "I wasn't doing anything bad."

He scoffed and finished his doughnut.

"Why did you even want me here? What do you want from me?"

He opened a cardboard box sitting on the desk, pulled out a doughnut, and handed it over to me, wrapped up in a napkin. "I want us to talk."

"I told you, I'm not interested in doing therapy with you or anyone else."

He sat down on the edge of the desk. "It's not therapy."

"Then, what is it?" I asked sarcastically.

"It's us, hanging out." He gestured to my doughnut. "We're conversing over a meal."

I rolled my eyes and ate my doughnut.

"Give me three meetings, like I asked, and that's it. I won't ask for anything more, but you promised."

"Fine, three visits. But if I don't want to talk about something, let it go."

"Got it." He hopped off the desk and stuck his hand out, and I grabbed it in mine. "Deal." Pulling away, he frowned at his now-sticky hand. "And you're already playing dirty."

I laughed, licking the glaze from my fingers. "I have a habit of playing dirty, Doctor."

I gulped, and my heart hammered in my chest when I realized it was about to start. This was going to happen. Weston was searching for the key to unlock my secrets, and as much as I protested it, curiosity pecked at my brain to see what he'd dig up.

He sat down, wiped off his hands, and stared at me with concentration. "Is there somewhere you'd like to start?"

This was a different man than the one I'd met three years ago. Weston had advanced into his career and grown.

"No," I drew out, squirming in my seat. "Not really."

His eyes locked with mine. "Rule number one: you need to be completely comfortable with me."

"You've seen me naked. I'm pretty comfortable with you," I said, faking a laugh. It was sad I'd rather a guy see me naked physically than emotionally.

"Yeah, I'm not searching for that type of comfortable."

I frowned.

"I want you to feel comfortable talking to me."

"I won't feel comfortable talking to you, considering *I don't want to* talk to you," I hissed. "I'm only here so you'll shut up."

"If you want to leave, then go ahead," he said, his voice turning agitated while he scratched his jaw. "I tried, but if you don't want my help, then go."

"It's that simple?"

"It's that simple, but don't call me again if you need help."

His response shocked me. That would be the easiest choice, right? I'd get up, walk out, and never talk to him again. So, why wasn't I doing that? Why was I still sitting here, staring at him?

"The fact that you're still here tells me a lot." He grinned wide, his bright white teeth showing. "Elise Parks, I think you want to talk to me."

I scowled. "One session. One. That's it. I'm only doing this because I paid for a cab ride here and don't want to waste my money."

"I'll take whatever reason you give me. Now that we have that over with, where do you want to begin? You can start talking. If you don't want to, I will. We'll play by your rules."

"Why are you doing this?"

"I want to help you get happy."

I wanted to tell him that would never happen. But I didn't. I stayed silent, not knowing what part of me I wanted to expose.

"Are you still doing drugs?" he asked, not even giving me the chance to think of my own conversation starter.

"No. I've been clean for a few years. I haven't taken an unprescribed pill since my last release."

His face lit up as a smile drew across his face. "Good. I'm proud of you." His smile fell. "Obviously, you're still drinking though."

"I hardly think that's a problem. Everyone I know drinks."

He stared at me with disapproval. I was sure I wasn't his only patient who drank underage. "Sure, but it's against the law."

"So, are you going to tell me you never drank before you were twenty-one?"

"I'm telling you, that's none of your business."

I rolled my eyes. "That tells me your answer. I'm not doing

drugs, but I still drink, and before you ask, yes, I still have sex." I paused. "Do you think I'm crazy?"

"I absolutely know you're not crazy."

I looked at him in disbelief. "Now, I know you're lying to make me feel better. I'm fucked up in the head. Nobody does the things I do or has thoughts in their head like I do without being fucked up."

"No one is truly *fucked up*, Elise. So, quit thinking that. Either you're being overdramatic or you've been severely misdiagnosed."

I snorted. "No one is truly fucked up?"

He nodded.

"John Gacy, Ted Bundy—"

"All right," he said, cutting me off from rambling off every serial killer I could think of. "Those people truly are 'fucked up in the head,' as you put it, but that's not you. As much as you can be a loose cannon at times and you make some stupid decisions"—he shook his head when I flipped him off—"you're still far from being a psychopath like them, and you know it."

"Then, how do you explain me?"

"You're confused. You're angry about something and acting out because of it."

I nodded in agreement.

"Why don't we start with what happened the other night before I picked you up?"

"Seriously?"

He held up his hands in surrender. "I didn't make you talk about it then."

I bit my fingernails, the bitter taste of the polish on my tongue. "I was over at my boyfriend's—well, now, ex-boyfriend's—house. I guess you could say, things went sour."

Sour. That was a decent word for the ass beating he had

given me. The sad thing was that I wasn't pissed about Oliver hitting me. I'd been hit before. I was mad that I hadn't had enough fight in myself to win. Every time I lost a battle, I was angry at myself.

"How long did you two date?"

"Only a few weeks." I wasn't sure if we'd even been dating. Our dates had consisted of going to dinner or a club, getting wasted, and then heading directly to his bed.

"So, not too long. How did you meet?"

"My father."

My father would only set me up with rich men with good names. Oliver was the son of an affluent man in Congress. Those were the only ones suitable for marriage in his eyes. Oliver was far from being suitable for marriage. He liked to fuck and party. That was about it. He'd never be a one-woman man.

"What happened?"

"I found a pair of cheap panties in his bed while riding him."

His back stiffened at my confession. He hadn't expected me to be so blunt.

"You'd better put on your seat belt for this roller coaster, Doctor. Me telling you about riding his cock isn't the worst of my story."

He blew out a breath and shifted in his chair. "I can handle whatever you want to share with me."

"Oliver couldn't even find a good excuse to argue with. He wanted to explain himself, convince me to believe his lies, but I told him to take me home, which he didn't want to do. So, he pinned me against the wall instead. When I tried to leave, he attacked me." I decided to leave out the part where he'd been on ecstasy. Weston would assume I had done it with him.

"Have you talked to him since the incident?"

"I saw him last night." I held up my hand to stop him when he gave me a look. "And I told him to leave me alone. He's called a few times, but I haven't answered. Screw that asshole."

"What did your father say when he saw your face?"

"That it was my fault."

"What?" he asked, unable to hold in the shock.

He was just getting a taste of the filthy secrets on my plate.

"According to my father, I attacked him because that's what Saint Oliver told him. He doesn't believe me because I'm a lying whore."

"Why would you have attacked him?"

I flicked my hand through the air. "It doesn't matter. It never matters."

"It does matter, Elise. You come to me, and you tell me the truth. I want to know everything. Every. Darn. Thing. You tell me your story. I want your happy chapters, your embarrassing chapters, and the dark, filthy chapters that you have under lock and key. I want the entire story, and you're going to give it to me. I'm relentless, but I will help you."

I gulped, focusing on my lap, and whispered, "There're some things I'm not ready to talk about."

"I know, and I'll wait." His voice was sincere. "Let's go into your family. Where's your mom?"

"She's dead. I never knew her."

"How did she die?"

"Who knows?"

"Care to elaborate?"

"I've never been told the actual cause. I've heard she took a shotgun to her mouth and blew her brains out. I've heard she overdosed on every drug possible. I've heard she ran off with some junkie and he murdered her. My father is the most creative storyteller in the world. But he can't stick to one."

If he drank whiskey, it was one story. If it was rum, it was another. His story depended on the liquid in his glass.

"How old were you when she died?"

"Four or five maybe."

"Do you remember anything about her?"

I wished I did. I'd racked my brain, pleading with myself to conjure up any memory of her, but I always came up short. I'd lie in bed and make up my own stories. She'd be there for me. She'd save me, the sweet little girl playing with her dolls in the devil's lair and take me away from him. But I'd given up that hope a long time ago.

"She used to braid my hair," I said, revealing the one vague memory I had of her.

He gestured to my hair, tied up in a loose braid and falling over my shoulder. "Is that why you keep it that way?"

"I guess."

"With your mom gone, your father raised you?"

I nodded. "Him and my nanny."

"Tell me about him."

"Malicious. Evil. Controlling."

"And why do you think your father is all of those things?"

I shrugged. "Because he is. I'm twenty years old and useless. I have no control of my own life. Anytime I bring up getting a job, he tells me a woman this pretty doesn't need to work. He thinks work corrupts women, and if I thought about getting one, he'd throw me out of my apartment. I got my place a year ago right across the hall from him. Anytime I stepped out of line, he would send me to Sun Gate, even if I was clean, so I'd know who was in control."

"Have you ever told him you want to live on your own? To end all contact with him?"

I nodded again.

"And?"

"He tells me no. He tells me I'll end up just like her. A dead whore."

"Has he always been this way?"

"As I can remember. He must approve all my friends."

Not that he was doing a good job since I got in more trouble with them.

"He needs to approve men I date," I continued. "Every one of them is an asshole. My father knows our relationship won't get serious. Which is fine for him because he doesn't want anyone to take me away from him unless he's getting something in return."

A knock on the door interrupted us, and an attractive blonde walked in. Her hair was tied into a bun at the base of her neck, and a black pantsuit covered her skinny figure.

"Hey, Wes," she said, her deep red lips smiling. "Sorry to interrupt you, but I have an appointment in five minutes. Next time, give me more of a heads-up, and I'll get you extra time."

Weston nodded. "That's fine. Thanks, Wendy."

She glanced over at me and gave me a tiny smile. I waited for her to say something, but she just stared before turning away and leaving the room.

"I'll see you tomorrow?" Weston asked, pushing himself up from the chair. "Come a little earlier, so we have more time."

"Why are you doing this?" I stood.

"I told you why. I want you to love yourself. My goal is for you to see your worth."

I tapped my head with the tip of my finger. "I've got some crazy stuff in here."

He stopped in front of me and reached up to smooth down my hair, his eyes casting down to meet mine. "I told you, I want it all." He poked my temple. "And that's what you're going to give me."

"Good luck. Figuring me out is like fighting off a gang of

pirates, surviving the Bermuda Triangle, and then catching a mermaid."

"I'm always up for a challenge."

eleven

ELISE

"You use sex and alcohol to numb yourself," Weston said. "I'm sure you know that. I'm also certain you know it's dangerous. Those men don't care about you. They only care about what you give them. After that, they can drop you off on the corner or kill you and throw you in a ditch or an abandoned alley."

I'd told myself last night I wouldn't come again today. I wasn't going to talk to him again. We'd had our one meeting, I'd told him how I felt, and that was it. But when he texted me this morning, telling me he had bagels and coffee, he somehow convinced me to come. Or at least, that had been my excuse to see him again.

I didn't want to tell him, but he was right. It was refreshing, almost liberating, to get everything out and not worry about him telling anyone. I could tell him my side of the story and be done with it.

I was also getting to know him just as well as he was me. I'd learned he didn't hold back. He wasn't afraid to speak the truth or call me out on my bullshit now.

"A lot of people use alcohol and sex to numb themselves. Sex gives people a high. It makes us feel better, whether drunk, in love, or out of love. People have sex romantically, casually, or sadistically. Either way, they do it because it gives them a rush. It gives them a high that makes them feel wanted—something they feel they need in that moment. Sex is not only for people who are in love."

I shook my head before going on. "Parents try to convince their children that they need to wait for love because they don't want them out, spreading their legs and fucking everyone in sight. Love is a joke. But eventually, they'll most likely have sex, and chances are, they won't love that person."

I thought back to the many men I'd willingly gone down on in dirty restroom stalls in random clubs and those who'd taken me home but never bothered to give me a ride or cab fare afterward. I'd never had sex with a man who cared about me because I'd never had a man care about me.

But I couldn't hold that against them. I knew what they were doing because I was playing the same game. I didn't take names. I threw out their business cards with the next day's trash. I didn't want their fraudulent dinners or their lies of affection. I wanted them to take my mind away temporarily, give me control, and then I discarded them. I was just as bad as they were.

"Wow, you sure do have a negative outlook on love," he said, pushing his sleeves up his arms. "Don't you think that's wrong?"

I shrugged, popping a bite of bagel in my mouth. "Not really. Look at you. You're not wearing a wedding ring, and I'd bet you're not a virgin. You probably know sex is enjoyable."

"Yes, I'm well aware that sex can be enjoyable," he said, failing to hold back a smile.

I grinned. "Does my doctor have a kinky side?"

My thoughts returned to sex with him like they had the night at his apartment. The guy fucked with people's minds for a living, so I'm sure he'd properly fuck a woman. And why was I constantly thinking about him fucking me?

He cleared his throat. "Talking about my sex life isn't why we're here. Let's stay on topic."

I crossed my arms, slightly leaning forward to give him a good view of my cleavage. "But talking about yours sounds like a lot more fun."

"Not everyone sees sex as a game." His voice was flat.

"I don't either. I have sex for power and control."

His eyebrows squeezed together. "Huh? Why? That makes no sense."

"I told you why three years ago."

"I know, but ..."

I clenched my jaw as my muscles jumped underneath my skin. "I was raped, Weston. Raped. If you don't believe me, that's fine. I honestly don't care who doesn't believe me anymore. I've moved on from it. I'll never forget what happened to me even with all the sex and alcohol in the world. I'm not a victim, I'm a survivor."

I never wanted to be seen as a victim, for people to know they'd hurt me. I'd hide behind a bad reputation before allowing that to happen.

Weston straightened his shoulders as surprise flashes in his eyes. He hadn't expected me to say that. "So, you have sex because you were raped? It makes you feel in control?"

I blew out a breath. "Yes."

He blinked at me, speechless.

"Some people break down after being violated. Some get angry. Some take charge and don't allow it to keep them down.

I decided to do the third choice. I didn't want to be the broken girl. That would mean they'd won. I've had too much taken away from me. I wouldn't give them that satisfaction. I don't get sad when I think about what those guys did to me. I get angry. I want to do anything to get my power back. Murder would've been my first option, but obviously, that would have put me in prison, so I found another way."

"I don't understand," Weston muttered, staring up at the ceiling and shaking his head. "I don't understand any of it."

I knew my situation was a total mindfuck that most people wouldn't be able to comprehend. I didn't understand it half of the time. "You don't understand it because you think I'm a liar."

He stared at me and struggled for words until finally clearing his throat. "Why weren't the cops called? Charges filed?"

"My father owns the cops. If he doesn't want something filed, it doesn't get filed."

"Why did everyone call you a liar?" He scrubbed his forehead.

"I tried to tell my truth, but everyone who tried to help was bribed or threatened to keep their mouths shut. They labeled me a liar, a girl searching for attention, so no one believed me." My stomach churned, and I was scared my bagel would come up. "My father ensured he was protected while making sure I wasn't."

My father was a very intelligent man. If my files were ever to be leaked, they would exhibit a pattern, and people with patterns couldn't be victims, right? It would show that I had a promiscuous background, was caught sleeping with an older man, a liar, so my word meant nothing."

She was asking for it, they said.

She was lying for attention, they added.

One night, I'd finally broken down and told the older man I slept with, Peter, what had happened to me. Peter lived in our building, and he told the police. The problem was, I was underage, and Peter admitted to sleeping with me, incriminating himself in the process.

The report was written, Peter was arrested, but my father gave him an offer he couldn't refuse. A one-of-a-kind plea deal, a check, to keep his mouth shut about anything I'd told him. When Peter was later questioned, he told them I'd admitted to lying about the rapes for attention. My father agreed with him, so they labeled me a liar."

Weston shifted in his chair. "It just doesn't make sense."

"It does. My father wanted people to think I was a liar, a slut, so he wouldn't be exposed. No one believes a whore, and they sure as hell don't care if bad things happen to them."

"Did you tell anyone before Peter?"

"I was too terrified. My father swore if I told anyone he'd have me admitted for the rest of my life—that is, if he didn't kill me for creating problems for him first." I blew out a breath. "I thought I finally had a chance with Peter, but it backfired on me." My eyes met his. "Did *you* tell anyone when I told you?"

"That's irrelevant now," he snapped, his face turning from curious to compassionate to anger.

The mood of the room suddenly shifted. Weston looked away from me.

Irrelevant? The hell it is.

"You didn't get fired, but I never saw you again. So, what happened?"

I was being honest with him. He needed to return the favor.

His eyes tightened around the corners, and he pulled at his hair. "They said you were lying, showed me your history, and said I was too inexperienced to work with you." He blew out a ragged breath, and his next words strangled from his throat. "You were ... you were really raped?"

"I can't believe you." My throat burned with anger that he was still questioning me. "You're like all the others—all men who don't believe me."

I grabbed my bag, ready to charge out of the room, but Weston jumped out of his chair to stop me.

"Please don't think I'm calling you a liar," he said, standing in front of me and resting his hands on my shoulders. "I only wanted to make sure you were honest with me."

"And there's a difference?" I asked coldly.

"There is. I'm trained in behavior. I'm trained to distinguish if someone is being honest or lying."

My head spun as I tried to pull away from his hold, but he held on tighter. My stomach churned with anger as I grew dizzier. "So, what does your oh-so-intelligent training say about me?"

His breathing lowered. I stared at him, begging him to meet my eyes, but he refused to look at me.

"You're not lying," he muttered, his eyes studying the floor. "You're telling the truth. I'm so sorry that happened to you."

His hands left my shoulders when I shoved him off.

"Then, there's your answer," I cried out. "I'm not a lying whore. Are you happy now? Did I convince you well enough?"

He winced at my words. "I never thought for one second that you were a lying whore."

"Could've fooled me."

I was being harder on him than I should've been, but I was so fed up with being questioned. I was tired of people not taking me seriously and thinking I was crying wolf for attention. I got enough attention. I'd had enough attention to last me the rest of my life.

"Tell me everything," he insisted, the couch indenting when he sat next to me.

I shook my head. "I can't. I'm not going back to that place."

"Yes, you can." His voice was soft ... soothing. "No one else will know what you told me. This is just you and me." He turned almost pleading. "Please trust me, Elise."

My lips trembled, and I hated that my eyes watered. "I don't trust anyone."

He shifted me to the side, bringing my head up to brush away the tears I wished I weren't shedding. "Let me prove it to you. Let me show you I'm trustworthy." He grabbed my hand. "I know you don't want to go back there, but you need to. *Open up to me.* Let me hear it. If it becomes too much, stop. But *please*, for the love of God, tell me what you can."

I took a few deep breaths and exhaled them before speaking, "I'll remember the first time until I die. My father was still working his way up the corporate ladder, building relationships with the highest execs in the city, and he wanted the world at his fingertips. While he strived for power, he realized I could be a useful asset."

"Son of a bitch," he mumbled.

"The first time was on my thirteenth birthday. I was sitting in front of my vanity and testing out the different lip glosses Bella, my nanny growing up, had gotten for me. He came in with a man I'd never seen before. I'll never forget the man's predatory eyes staring at me and sizing me up. They were icy but melted when my father told me to stand up. I wore a tank top and pajama pants with cherries printed on them. The man licked his lips and asked my father if he'd be the one to pop the cherry between my legs."

Weston drew in a sharp breath, his lips screwing into a grimace. He was fighting back his anger for my sake. He wanted to hear everything before releasing it.

"I didn't understand his words, but that didn't stop me from being terrified. My father told him yes as long as he stuck with the deal. The man scanned me over again before shaking my father's hand. My father told the man he had thirty minutes, and then I watched the man who was supposed to protect me leave me alone with this scary stranger. I didn't even realize what was happening until he took his pants off and demanded I do the same. He threw me on my bed. I thought I'd vomit at the feel of his heavy body crawling over mine. I did everything he told me to do because I was scared to say no."

I wished I'd fought back. I replayed that day in my head thousands of times, thinking maybe if I had told him no or screamed out for help, it wouldn't have happened. But I hadn't. I'd stayed quiet and followed his orders.

Weston's body brushed against mine when he grabbed a tissue and started wiping my face. "Do you want to stop?" he asked, collecting my tears.

I shook my head. There was no turning back now. "It was painful. I cried the entire time. He touched me for a few minutes, telling me he wanted to get me wet, before flipping me on my stomach and dragging my knees up. I didn't look back at him once. I cried out as pain ricocheted through my body while this man slammed in and out of me. He grunted like a dying animal while he raped me, and after what seemed like an eternity, he was done."

"You're doing great," Weston said, sweeping away the strands of hair that had fallen in my face, sticking to my tears.

I choked out another sob. My voice shook. My body shook. Every piece of me shook. "The man told me I was now a woman and left the room. I stayed on my bed, naked and curled into a ball, waiting for my father to come save me. But he never came. He left me alone. So, I lay there and cried. I cried until I felt like I had nothing left inside me. Later that night, I snuck into my father's office, grabbed a handful of matches, and set my bed on fire." I snorted. "That became a ritual of ours. He'd sell me off and know he'd have to buy me a new bed after I set mine to flames."

I lost the warmth of Weston's hand when he pushed up from the couch, grabbed a book, and threw it across the room in a fit of rage.

"And—" I began to elaborate, not sure what else to do.

"That's enough for today," he said, cutting my words off quickly and pacing in front of me.

"But I thought you wanted—"

He inhaled a sharp breath. "That's enough for today. I can't believe this!" He threw another book, that one smashing against the wall. "How long did this go on?"

"Until I was seventeen."

It was embarrassing I'd allowed for it to go on that long, but I didn't know how to stop it. So, I let it continue to happen, feeling like I had no other options or anyone to turn to. I'd let the guys come like a revolving door.

His dark eyes narrowed at me. "Did it happen after we met?"

I nodded. "Just once, but it wasn't exactly rape. I allowed it to happen because my father had insisted I show a man around the city and entertain him for the night."

His chair fell to the side when he kicked it.

I stared at him in shock. His hands trembled when he stalked my way and bent in front of me.

"Why are you so angry?" I whispered.

His head fell forward, his hands resting on my knees. "I could've stopped it."

I shook my head. "No, you couldn't have."

He stared at me with sorrow in his eyes. "Let's stop for today, okay?"

"Okay," I drew out.

He was disgusted with me. He didn't see me as the strong woman anymore.

"I'll call a cab," I said.

"No," he said, bringing himself up. "Let me take you to lunch."

I blinked. "What?"

"You need to clear your head. Let's go get some lunch—my treat."

"I don't feel like going out like this." I gestured to my face. "I'm a hot mess."

"We'll order in. Give me a sec."

I nodded, and he left the room.

I grabbed a handful of tissues to clean my face and opened my purse for my compact to check my reflection. I looked terrible. Black mascara marks lined my cheeks. I scrubbed at them with a tissue, removing the makeup, which caused my bruises to resurface.

"Quit it. You look beautiful," Weston said, coming back into the room with a handful of takeout menus.

He handed them to me, and I flipped through the menus before deciding.

"Chinese. Good choice," he said. "I'll be right back."

Ten minutes later, he returned with a bag in his hand. "I ordered nearly everything on the menu, so I hope there's something you like here." His lips formed a weak smile as he held the bag in the air.

"Thank you. I love Chinese," I answered.

We settled on the carpet, and he sprawled out the containers of food, sauces, and drinks before handing me a plate and chopsticks.

We ate in silence until I finally cleared my throat. "Why did you decide to do this for a living?"

He shrugged, playing with his food. "It's personal."

I snorted. "God forbid we share anything personal with each other."

He set down his chopsticks and scrubbed a hand over his face. "I had a twin brother, Wale. He was my best friend and so full of life as a kid. But something in him changed when we got to high school. He felt like a social outcast, like he didn't belong. He became jealous of my sister and me. I made better grades than him. I became class president. He ran for vice president and lost. My parents bragged about my achievements but paid no attention to his. He felt like he was never good enough. I tried to make him feel better, even failed a few tests so my GPA would drop, and it worked for a few months."

His shoulders curled forward. "But everything changed when he didn't get accepted into Columbia. Our family had attended that college for generations. That hit him hard. He got into drugs and started drinking. He didn't care about his life. I tried to talk sense into him, but he shut me out."

I bit my lip, shocked at his truth, but the more he talked, the more comfortable I became.

Weston rubbed his eyes before staring at the floor, as if those memories were hitting him in real time. "I left for college, and he moved to Michigan after meeting a girl at a bar who lived there. He called me one night, the day before my finals, acting strange, and said his girlfriend cheated on him. He cried that he hated his life and couldn't take it anymore. He'd talked about ending his life before, but this time, it was different. His tone, his words, everything was different."

When he peered back up at me, his eyes were glazed over. "I jumped on the first flight to Michigan. I knew he was going to do something stupid. But I was too late. He'd hung himself in his apartment closet."

My hand flew to my mouth, and I whimpered.

He squeezed his eyes shut. "After his death, I went through his things and found his journal. It was so damn raw. It was heartbreaking reading about what had been going on in his mind. He'd had depression, hysteria, an undiagnosed mental disorder, but he'd never sought help." His shoulders slumped, as if he was running out of energy to speak. "After reading every entry, I changed my major. I decided I was going to help people like him. It might've been too late to save him, but I could help someone else during their fight and let them know things would get better. If I could save a life, that's what I'd do. I wouldn't allow his death to mean nothing."

"Wow," I said, gazing up at him.

This man, he was one of the sweetest, down-to-earth guys I knew.

Realistically, he was the only good guy I knew.

"You're a good guy," I whispered.

He grabbed his chopsticks, his hold on them so tight I was waiting for them to break and pointed to me with them. "Eat."

I picked at my chow mein. "I'm sorry about your brother."

"Thank you. He was a great guy. You would've liked him."

"Was he cute?" I asked, getting him to crack a smile.

He chuckled, shaking his head at me. "If you think I'm cute, then you would've thought he was."

"Oh yeah, twins." I faked annoyance. "Maybe he would've shared his sex stories with me since his boring brother won't."

"Oh, you would've scared him." A hint of a smile his hit lips, which made me smile. "Your beauty would've transfixed him. I'm sure he wouldn't have been able to mutter three words to you."

"What about you?" A rush of shyness—something I hadn't experienced in a long time—hit me. "Do you think I'm pretty?"

He peered at me, his gaze deep, and didn't answer until we held eye contact for seconds "I think you're a beautiful."

I blushed.

"Inside and out," he added. He dropped his napkin and reached forward to rub his thumb over a bruise on my cheek. "You're very beautiful, Elise. Don't let anyone tell you any different."

twelve

ELISE

"How have you been?" my father asked from across the table.

He'd insisted we go out to dinner in the city. We needed to show everyone that I was a better person and wasn't out, causing chaos. The world also needed to know that we got along and had a healthy relationship. He was tired of being questioned about me. The focus needed to be on him and his companies, not on whether I was on my latest rehab stint or dancing on a bar without a top on.

"Good," I replied, playing with the napkin in my lap.

I ignored the stares, restraining myself from flipping off every nosy diner ogling us. We were at a five-star restaurant, but that didn't mean people had manners and minded their business. It was worse. Wealthy people loved their juicy gossip.

"I heard you're going to therapy." he went on. "I thought you hated therapy?"

I shrugged and took a drink of water before answering him. "I wanted to try something different."

I had known he'd find out I'd been visiting Wendy's office. I

76

wasn't sure how he managed to track my every move, but it annoyed me.

"I'm unhappy I wasn't aware of this before you made the appointment." He took a drink of wine and then dabbed his lips with the cloth napkin. "What have you told this new therapist?"

I leveled my gaze on him and snarled in his direction. "Don't worry, Daddy. I'll keep your secrets and abuse quiet."

He gaped at me. "Abuse? What are you talking about? I've never abused you."

I dropped my fork, and it banged loudly against my plate. "Are you kidding me?" My mouth went dry, a bitter taste forming.

He was going to flip this around on me like he always did. Somehow, he'd make it appear like I'd wanted to be raped.

"Don't you ever say that in public again," he warned. "Do you hear me?" His lips pinched together while he tried to keep his composure in check. We had to convey the happy family that we'd never be.

I glanced down at my barely eaten food. I couldn't stand even looking at him.

"Just like I had with your mother, I've given you a great life, Elise. My money has sent you to get help in very expensive places. Everything I do and I've done has been for you." His face turned rigid as he leaned in closer. "I don't ever want you to worry about money or working. You've started moving forward, keeping your mouth shut, and I'm proud of you."

"And I haven't done my part?" I sneered. "You wouldn't have that money without pimping me out to your scumbag associates."

"I greatly appreciate what you've done for this family."

"How sweet that you appreciate my abuse for your benefit."

"That's not abuse," he argued.

"You let men rape me," I hissed. "You sold out my virginity to the highest bidder."

"Elise, my sweet, you wanted it," he disputed, his tone almost taunting. "You've been caught sleeping with multiple men and enjoy sex, so what's the difference? We might as well get something out of it."

"I didn't like it when I was thirteen," I said, each word catching in my throat before releasing it.

"Thirteen but wearing makeup and miniskirts. You were hardly a teenager and already dressing like a little slut."

"I was still a virgin."

He clasped his hands in front of him and moved closer into my space. "How many men have you willingly slept with? You like it. Now, shut up and finish your dinner." He sighed in annoyance. "I wanted us to have an enjoyable meal."

I tried to keep my cool, but I wasn't sure how long that would last. "Take me home."

"Absolutely not." He pointed to my plate with his fork. "Finish your dinner."

"I don't have an appetite."

"And I don't care." He grabbed his glass and took a drink of his overpriced wine. "I haven't seen you in a week, and you don't answer my phone calls, so you're going to sit there and spend time with your father."

"Too bad I don't enjoy spending time with you."

His hand tightened around his glass. I briefly noticed his eyes grow glossy, but they instantly heated when he came to his senses. Even though he tried to hide it, I knew my rejection hurt him.

"You are the only thing I have, baby girl." He roughly adjusted his tie. "You will never leave me, so get used to it. I will chain you to your goddamn room if I have to, but I will not allow you to turn out like your mother."

"How can I turn out like her if I don't even know her?"

"You want to know her?" he asked, stroking his throat.

"Yes, I do." *More than anything. Well, other than my freedom.*

"She was a whore," he said, straightforward, no bullshit.

I shook my head in disbelief. "That's not true." I was tired of him constantly calling her that. "You loved her."

"When we met, it was because your mother was paid to fuck me," he seethed. "Is that what you wanted to hear?"

My stomach dropped in disgust. No, I didn't want to hear about my father having sex, and I most definitely wished I hadn't heard what he'd just told me.

"You're lying," I whisper, staring down at my lap.

He had to be lying.

"It was my birthday, and my father bought me a hooker as my gift." He released a cruel laugh—one you'd hear from villains in the movies. "That's right; your mother was a paid whore, and she was good at it. She excelled at sex. But she wasn't like any hooker out there. She was exceptionally beautiful, striking." He slammed his eyes shut, as if he was taking a moment to remember her. "She catered to me the entire night, like I was her king. So, I rented her the next night, eventually becoming a regular customer until I finally begged her to quit that life and be my wife. Your grandfather was furious and cut me off. I gave up everything for her."

He took another long pull of wine, and I knew where this was going. Like me, my father couldn't stomach talking about his problems without having a high.

"But I had to have her," he hissed, fire in his eyes. "I loved that woman more than I loved breathing. She was my everything. I took her off the streets and bought her everything she could ever want. I worked my ass off to give her the life she dreamed of. And you know what she gave me in return?" He paused, taking another drink. "She fucked my best friend. And my *father*."

"You're lying," I repeated around a gasp, trying to wrap my head around what I'd just been told.

That wasn't my mother. She wouldn't have done that. She hadn't been this horrible person he was describing.

He stared at me with sorrow. "I wish I were."

"If you hate whores so much, why did you marry her?"

"Because I loved her. She promised she'd change, but she couldn't stop. She loved that life."

A silence passed between us, and when I spoke, my voice was hoarse. "Did you kill her?"

He winced at my question ... accusation ... whatever it was. "I would never, never have hurt your mother. I loved her, and she left me." He lowered his tone. "I was pissed, but I could never have hurt her." His hand lightly hit the table. "I loved the stupid bitch. She ran off with another man and returned to tricking on the streets. She craved the nightlife and couldn't let it go. She left me and ended up dead." He slumped his shoulders, appearing almost vulnerable and nothing like my normal father. "Do you understand why I don't want you out there? I couldn't save her, but I'll be damned if I let you turn out like her. You have her blood in you. If you ever went out on your own, you'd do the same thing. I can't let that happen. I can't lose you. You're all that I have left."

I stared at him, speechless. My mind rambled with questions, but my mouth wouldn't open. What the hell was I supposed to say to that? He'd never opened up about her.

I took a few deep breaths before I choked up the nerve to speak. "I'm not like her."

"I can't trust you. I trusted her and look what happened." He violently shook his head. "I did everything to make her change, but that wasn't good enough. She ended up back with her pimp, and he stabbed her fifteen times before throwing her dead body on the side of the highway."

And there it was—the truth about my mother. She had been a hooker, a whore, and she was dead because her pimp had killed her. I no longer had an appetite. I needed a drink.

"I don't get it," I said. "You say you don't want me to be a whore, but you let guys screw me for business deals. Isn't that the same thing?" I didn't want to say it, but in reality, he was my pimp.

"There's nothing for you to get. It happened a few times, Elise," he said, motioning to the server for the bill. "I wish you'd just forget about it and move on."

Unless they'd been violated, people didn't understand moving on wasn't easy.

thirteen

ELISE

"You look lonely over here. Can I buy you a drink, gorgeous?" the raspy voice asked from behind me, breaking me away from my thoughts of misery.

All I could think about on my way to the bar was what my father had revealed.

I'd had this naive misconception of my mom being this wonderful woman my father had destroyed. But I'd had it all wrong. It was the other way around. She'd destroyed him. He was the way he was because of her. Her selfish actions had caused him to hate the world and me. I detested her for that.

My father hadn't muttered another word to me on the drive home. As soon as I walked through my front door, I stripped out of my clothes, changed into a formfitting black dress, and snuck out into the night. I'd needed to get the hell out of there.

The guy slid into the barstool next to mine without waiting for my answer. A suggestive smile was on his face when I finally turned to focus on him. His hair was styled into the perfect Ivy League haircut, showing off his clean-shaven face. He was sexy with a broad chest and defined muscles. I was certain he'd been physically active his entire life, but with something more along the lines of tennis or rowing. He was slightly younger than Weston, probably around twenty-four.

He was exactly my type—or my old type, considering I was crushing on my shrink who wore glasses and dressed like a hobo most of the time.

"I don't know. Can you?" I fired back, wrapping my hand around my glass and taking a drink.

He was the fifth man who'd offered to buy me a drink tonight. The other four had bailed after discovering I wouldn't let them into my panties.

Can I buy you a drink was the laziest pickup line in the history of pickup lines. It was the polite way of asking if they could get you piss drunk and then fuck you in the backseat of their car. It was a sleazeball move. I mean, what was easier than paying a few bills for a drink? It was cheaper than dinner and a movie and usually ended with a better bang. Literally.

He signaled to the bartender. "Another of whatever the lady is drinking."

The brooding bartender eyeballed me in question with each drink purchased by a stranger and followed his instruction.

The man swiveled in his chair and rested his elbow on the bar to lock eyes with me. "Do you have a name?"

I raised a brow. "I do."

"And what might that be?"

"Elise."

He shook his head, rubbed his hand down his smooth cheek, and paused for a moment, like he was about to give great thought to his next words. "Elise—that's a beautiful name."

That's a beautiful name?

His lack of creativity disappointed me.

I shrugged. "It was a birthday present."

He laughed, his bright white teeth glowing in the dim lights from behind the bar. "Why don't you tell me about yourself?"

"There's not much to tell."

"I disagree. You're a gorgeous girl, sad, and sitting alone at a bar on a Thursday night. There's a story. There's always a story."

There was a story, but he sure as hell wouldn't be hearing it.

"Nope," I said.

The bartender set my drink down in front of me.

"Let me guess." The guy's finger went to his lips. "A breakup?"

I shook my head.

"A fight with the boyfriend?"

I shook my head again. "No boyfriend."

"Your friend in the restroom, getting fucked?"

Another head shake.

"Or did she bail on you to get some dick?"

He laughed as I shot him an annoyed glare.

"No friend getting rammed in the restroom."

I'd called Holly to come out with me tonight, but she'd said she wasn't going out if Quinton couldn't come, and that wasn't happening.

"So, no boyfriend or friend?" He clicked his tongue against the roof of his mouth. "It's probably not smart to hang out at a bar alone."

I watched him slide the rim of his glass along his lips, take a long drink, and then set it back on the bar. I gulped. This guy was good. I was sure he had girls begging to sleep with him.

"I'm not sleeping with you," I blurted out, not wanting him to get his hopes up.

"Well, that's a bummer," he replied, his smile wider.

I was stupid. I'd been promoted from an easy lay to a challenge now.

He raised his chin. "How about you get to know me before you make that call?"

"I don't want to know you."

"Give me five minutes." He held out his hand. "I'm Vincent Peterson. It's nice to meet you."

I rolled my eyes at the mention of his name and ignored his hand. He was a man who used his notoriety to get him laid. His family owned an international beer distribution company and a few state sports teams. They were loaded—old money.

"I'm sorry, but your name is not so beautiful," I said bluntly.

I'd slept with two other Petersons—possibly a cousin, brother, or someone like that. They were nothing to brag about and all about themselves in the bedroom.

He downed the rest of his drink. "Oh, come on. Don't use that against me."

I blinked at him. "Do you know who I am?"

He nodded, a twinkle of amused interest flashing in his eyes. "I do."

"And?"

"You're supposedly the out-of-control daughter of Clint Parks. But I have to say, I'm a little disappointed."

"Why is that?"

"I don't see any erratic behavior here. I'm waiting for you to get on the bar and start dancing in that short little dress you have on ... or do body shots off me." A smirk grew on his lips. "Which I can arrange, by the way."

"So, is that why you approached me?" I frowned. "You know who I am and my reputation?"

"Probably." There was no shame or apology in his reply.

I had to give him credit for his honesty.

He pointed at me. "At first, I wanted to see what all the hype was about, but now, I'm intrigued by you for some reason."

"I intrigue you?" I repeated with a sarcastic laugh. "You

don't even know me. I'm still not going to sleep with you, even after hearing your last name."

He grinned.

"So, stop with the ridiculous pickup lines."

"You don't know if that's what I want. I haven't said anything to you about getting into your panties."

"I know that face. Your entire family makes that face when they want their dick sucked."

"Wow, that's embarrassing." He threw his head back and laughed. "I'll be sure never to make this face again."

"Yeah, I'd be embarrassed too."

"So, you don't want me to judge you, yet you're judging me? I promise, I'm nothing like my family *in and out* of the bedroom."

"Too bad I won't be finding out."

What was wrong with me? Why wasn't I jumping at this guy's advances? Why wasn't I opening my legs wide, as a sign I wanted his hand there? He'd be the perfect screw to get my mind off Weston.

"You sure about that?" he asked.

"I am."

He groaned. "All right then." He tucked his hand into his pocket to pull out a business card. "If you ever change your mind, call me." He handed it over. "You've got something to you, Elise Parks, and I'd be very interested to find out what that is." He threw down a few bills on the bar before leaving.

"Wait," I said, turning around in my chair.

"Yes?" he asked, flashing me a smile. "Please tell me you've changed your mind?"

His smile dropped when I shook my head.

"Can I get a ride?" I dramatically fluttered my lashes.

It was freezing outside. I didn't want to walk home, and hailing a cab sounded like a headache.

"Are you serious?" He glowered at me. "Is this a game? You want that ride to come back to my place?"

I bit the edge of my lip. "Can I get a ride *home*?"

He stared at me in shock. "You just turned me down which means I need to find another way to get out my frustrations."

I rolled my eyes. "Ugh, whatever." *Typical.*

Like all the other men who'd left, he was just hunting for his next one night stand. The embarrassing thing was that I used to fall for it.

"But I will tell my driver to take you." He pulled out his phone. "He'll be out front, waiting for you whenever you're ready. It was nice meeting you, Elise. I hope to see you again in the future."

With that, he walked through the crowd searching for his next conquest.

fourteen

ELISE

I stumbled into my bedroom, tripping on my heels, and fought with myself to kick them off after Vincent's driver dropped me off. I used my dresser as leverage to clumsily shed my clothes, nearly falling on my face in the process, and then finally threw myself into bed. I snatched my phone, swinging my legs back and forth along the foot of the bed, and listened to it ring on the other line.

"Weston! My friend! My boy!" I shouted into the speaker as soon as he answered. My head swirled while I grabbed the vodka bottle on my nightstand. I'd been sipping on it while I got ready earlier.

"Elise?" He sounded irritated.

I glanced over at my alarm clock and noticed the time.

Two in the morning.

Well, shoot, time flies when you're getting wasted.

"That's me," I yelped around a giggle. *What the hell?* I wasn't a giggler. I swirled my tongue along the bottle's rim before taking a quick drink, and my voice turned excited. "I forgot how much I love vodka. Vodka is seriously my best friend. If I could, I'd marry vodka, and we'd have beautiful little vodka babies."

"Fuck me," he groaned.

Fuck him? Oh, I would gladly participate in that activity.

"You're wasted."

"Sure am," I chirped, hiccupped, and then took another drink. "And I'm just getting started."

Okay, *just getting started* was a bit of an understatement, but I needed to erase all the bombs that had been dropped on me during dinner.

He let out a frustrated sigh. "I know today was hard on you, but you should've called me before drinking yourself into a stupor."

He was going to hang up on me. No one ever had fun being the sober person, dealing with the drunken asshole. I'd personally never been in that position, but I was sure it wasn't a good time.

I felt like a child being scolded while I played with the bottle in my hand. "You have no idea what today or tonight was like for me," I stuttered. "No freaking idea."

"Then, why don't you tell me about it?" His voice turned gentle, and therapist Weston emerged from the shadows.

I took a deep breath before telling him, "My father talked about my mom tonight." My words ran into each other, sounding like one. "She is dead. All along, I thought maybe she was out there, waiting for me to find her. But, nope, she's really gone."

"I'm sorry to hear that." His tone turned more comforting.

"You know what's funny though? She was a whore, just like me," I said in amusement, taking another drink.

"I don't think that's true or funny," he replied flatly.

"She was a whore! I'm a whore! We're all whores!"

"Jesus Christ," he muttered. "You're not a whore, but you're acting like an idiot right now. Go to the kitchen and drink some water."

I swung the bottle back and forth in front of me, watching the liquid splash in fixation. "Nope, if it ain't vodka, I ain't drinking it."

"Get your ass in the kitchen, or I'm coming over there and doing it myself."

I perked up, my back going straight along my headboard, and sparks ran through my body as a sly smile spread over my lips. "Oh, really? Then, come right over."

"I'm hanging up now," he said, clearly catching on to my intentions.

"Wait," I said, rushing my word out. "You told me to call you if I ever needed anything."

"I'm beginning to think you misinterpreted the meaning of that."

I hadn't misinterpreted anything, but I had no problem acting like I did. I leaned sideways and carefully set the vodka bottle back in its place. I coasted along my sheets, feeling the Egyptian cotton trail along my skin, and made myself comfortable.

I exhaled a frenzied breath as I extended my hand down my belly, stopping at the hem of my boy shorts.

Am I about to do this?

Yes, I am.

"I need something," I said, my voice raspy.

"And what is that?"

"An orgasm."

And it was confirmed. I was truly batshit crazy. I was attempting—yes, seriously attempting—to seduce my psychologist. I wanted to have phone sex with him. *I really* wanted to have sex with him in person, riding his cock until I got what I needed. But phone sex would suffice.

It was wrong, and I knew that, but I hadn't been able to get Weston out of my head since the night he'd cut my dress off my body. I'd lie in bed, reliving that night in his bathroom, and touch myself to the copious illusions of what could've happened. I'd visualize my hands as his, pleasuring myself until I orgasmed against my fingertips.

He cleared his throat. "And I think it's time for us to say good night. Drink some water, take two Advil, and call me in the morning."

The room started spinning, the alcohol mixing with the thrill of what I wanted, and I slowly began to massage my clit over my panties. "Men wanted to sleep with me tonight, but I didn't give in. I didn't go home with one. You want to know why?"

The only sound from the other end was his heavy breathing.

"Because I wanted you to be the one who got me off. I didn't want some random guy from the bar playing with my pussy. I wanted it to be you."

"Take a cold shower." His voice was strained with conflict.

"Any other options more enjoyable?"

"Relieve yourself. You have fingers and, I'm sure, a vibrator somewhere around there. I can't help you with your problem."

"I'm not asking you to touch or fuck me. I'm asking you to talk to me."

The taste of vodka swept through my mouth while I worked myself with my fingers, playing with my tiny nub, and my urge for him to give in elevated. I needed more, but I patiently waited for him to join me before I went further. I wanted him to do this with me.

"Isn't that what your job is?" I asked. "Isn't that what you ordered me to do? Talk to you when I needed help with my problems?"

I bucked my hips forward when I buried my hand into my

panties. The drama from the night began to fade away when I felt how wet I was as I caressed my slit.

"I'm sorry," he whispered. "I can't do this."

"Do you know how much I want you?" I needed to up the ante. I wasn't giving up. "I'm already touching myself. My fingers are in my panties. I've been playing with myself for days, thinking about you."

He panted from the other side of the call.

Mission accomplished.

I put the phone on speaker and positioned it next to my mouth. "I've dreamed about us together," I said, eliciting a moan. "I envision your hands all over my body, touching me everywhere, and how amazing we'd feel, skin to skin. I haven't slept with anyone since I started seeing you. Do you want to know why?"

"Why?" he stammered, and I knew I was getting to him.

"Because the thought of someone else inside me makes me sick to my stomach. It makes my skin crawl. You should be the one inside me, not anyone else."

Shit, my own words were enough to set me off. Alcohol was making me one vocal bitch. I would've never admitted that while sober. Drunken minds spoke sober thoughts.

I used my free hand to pull down my bra, and my nipple hardened when I kneaded my breast. Using my other hand, I dragged my juices along my slit, and the tips of my fingers slid along my opening until I couldn't take it any longer. I wasn't a stranger to getting myself off. I knew how I liked it.

"I'm so wet," I confessed with a moan.

I'd never wanted something so badly. I desperately ached to push a finger inside my throbbing heat, but I held back, waiting for him to play this game with me. I gritted my teeth, failing at suppressing a loud moan when I spread my legs wider and finally slipped a finger inside.

This would happen whether he wanted to participate or not.

"I can't do this," he croaked out. "I can't do this."

"Are you telling me you've never thought about it before?" I asked. "You've never thought about bending me over that desk and pounding inside me?"

"This can't happen," he ground out, warring with himself on what to do. "I can't do this."

I already knew his answer. He would've hung up long ago if he didn't want to play along. I just needed to give him that pushing start.

"Technically, I don't *pay* you for your services. So, we don't have to call you *my* psychologist," I said, my breathing faltered. "I'm a woman, and you're a man. We're attracted to each other. It's as simple as that."

"Goddamn it," he growled.

Silence hung between us, and I held back a squeal when he broke it.

"This can never come up."

"Never." An electric jolt sparked through me, and I realized this would happen. Excitement fizzled along my hand as I moved my finger in and out of myself.

"If you want this with me, you have to listen, okay?"

"Anything," I moaned out.

I'd never wanted somebody inside me so desperately as I did him. I wasn't sure if it was because he was so forbidden or because he'd found something in me nobody else had, but I was salivating with obsession over this man.

"Are you wearing panties?"

"Yes."

"Are your fingers in your panties? Are you playing with your pretty little pussy right now?"

Holy shit. Weston had a filthy little mouth on him.

"Yes."

"Take them out," he demanded.

I froze, frowning. "What? I swear to God," I spat, "you'd better not be messing with me."

If he was playing some sick, twisted game, I would stomp right over to Wendy's office and burn the building down.

He chuckled. "I'm not, but you must listen to me if you want to play. I promise I'll make you feel good."

I wasn't sure how I felt about that. I'd never allowed a man I willingly had sex with to dictate how we were fucking. I'd never been submissive in the bedroom because of what had happened to me. I'd tell them how to fuck me. I'd tell them how to touch me. The saying *I have the pussy, so I make the rules* was my personal mantra. So, I wasn't sure how to react to his commands.

"Do it," he said harshly. "Drag your fingers out of your pussy, or I'm hanging up."

My pussy throbbed when I pulled my fingers out of my panties and rested them on my stomach. "Fine, fingers gone. You happy?"

"That's my good girl. Now, rub one finger across your wet clit."

What the hell? That was what I had just been doing.

"Over your panties," he added.

If I wasn't so turned on, I would've told him to fuck off, but I followed his directions. I'd do anything for this man at the moment. I brushed a shaking hand over my panties, shivering as the coarse fabric rubbed against my clit. I moved three fingers back and forth along my core, my body aching for more.

"Are you doing what I said?"

"Yes," I groaned, increasing my speed.

The material of my panties and the friction of my fingers

grinding on my clit felt exhilarating. I kicked the blanket off to focus on my hand.

"Does it feel good?"

"God, yes, so good." It felt better than good. It felt electrifying. I continued to feel the strong jolts kick through my body. "More," I panted. "Give me more." My mouth fell open when I put more pressure on my clit.

"Run your hand along the edge of your panties, then slowly dip it in. Touch yourself. I want you to feel how bad you want me. I want you to see how wet I make you."

Fire scorched in the pit of my stomach, and my fingers went to work to put it out.

"How wet do I make you?" he asked.

"I'm soaked," I moaned, shocked I could even speak. *It feels so good.* My fingers gained momentum. "Can I put it in?"

"Are you aching for me to be inside you?"

The man knew how to play mind games.

I zoned in on him, listening to his breathing, and my arousal instantly peaked. *Oh my God.* He was playing with himself. He was jacking himself off to me. I was sure of it.

"Are you jacking off?" I asked, unable to hold back my curiosity.

I knew if he said yes, it would be over. I'd be off in a matter of seconds with the mental image of him sprawled out on his bed, his pajama pants down to his knees, while he stroked himself wildly. My fingertips went numb while I waited for his answer.

"Yes," he croaked. "I'm jerking off, thinking about you playing with your wet pussy for me. I'm imagining what you'd feel like, how slick you'd be around my cock, and how you'd taste on my tongue."

"Do you have a big cock?"

He chuckled. "Mystery is captivating, baby. Now, slide a

finger into your tight pussy as I kiss your neck, tracing my lips up and down your smooth collarbone."

I pushed my middle finger inside myself, my breath catching in the back of my throat.

"I'm playing with you right now. I can feel every inch of you. You're so wet. So tight," he went on.

I added another finger without asking for permission. I drew it along the inside of my soft folds and anxiously plunged it in and out.

"Do you like me fingering you?"

"God, yes." I quivered, my body vibrating with each stroke.

His breathing was labored, his grunts coming out in long intervals that matched mine, and we let our imaginations take over.

"Am I fingering you hard or slow?"

"Hard. So damn hard." I increased my speed, gliding in and out of myself like it was my job and I needed a raise.

"Do you wish my dick were inside you? Sinking deep inside you and making you feel good?"

"I wish your big cock were inside me right now," I gasped, my body firing up at our words.

I was ready. I could feel the tingles multiplying through my body and shooting straight to my core. I didn't want to be ready, I wanted this to last forever, but my body couldn't take it anymore.

"You're getting there," he said. "Now, play with your clit."

"Are you almost there?" I asked, moving my hand away from my breast, pushing it down to my panties until I reached my clit. I didn't want to leave him behind, but I wasn't sure how much longer I'd be able to last.

"My strokes are getting faster. I'm almost there, baby. God, yes," he grunted. "You're so tight, so tight with my cock pumping in and out of you."

I wanted all of that.

"I want to feel all of you," I moaned.

"You got it all. You feel it?"

I slammed my eyes shut, the room growing dizzy while my imagination went wild. "Yes, you're inside so deep."

"You're so tight."

I was so wet. I could feel it with every slip as I dripped onto my sheets.

"You're going to get off now, you hear me? I'm there in your bed, our bodies slapping together, my sweat dripping on your big, delicious breasts, and I'm going to get off inside you."

His words were killing me. My lungs decided they were ready to give out, and all the blood rushed from my heart, through my belly, and between my legs. My body trembled as it came down from its high.

Drunken phone sex with Weston was more intense than real sex with anyone else.

My entire body tingled with waves of pleasure. He groaned a few times, and then a long growl escaped his throat as he let out his release.

"Holy shit," I said around a breath. "I guess you do have a kinky side."

I wanted more of it.

"This never happened," he said quickly.

And my high completely crashed down.

"This never happened," I squeaked out, trying to keep my voice level so he wouldn't sense my disappointment. "I promise I won't tell anyone," I added, blinking as I grew sleepy.

"Sleep tight."

And the line went dead.

I slammed my hands down against the bed. "Such a stupid girl," I muttered. "Stupid-stupid girl."

My head screamed at myself as I tossed and turned the rest

of the night. I'd given Weston the reins over my body, my orgasm, and my mind. I'd never done that with anyone. Then, he'd gotten off and left me. Just like the rest of them.

Only this time, I didn't try to fight it. I only wanted more.

I'd let him have it. I had given him a piece of me, and he'd stomped on it.

Is that how you feel when you're falling for someone and they're not there to catch you?

fifteen

ELISE

"Mother of God," I croaked, whipping my hand out from underneath my blanket, feeling around on my nightstand.

I ignored the bottle of vodka and sighed with relief when I found an old water bottle. I leisurely removed the cap, brought the rim to my lips, and took a sideways sip. I ignored the drizzle running down my chin and onto my pillow. There was no way in hell I was getting up yet. My head would topple over and fall at my feet.

I groaned, pressing my blanket over my face when I heard the antagonizing sound of my phone ringing. I spewed a string of curse words at it until it went silent.

"Thank you, Jesus," I grumbled.

When it started to ring again, I slapped my bed and tapped around until I found it.

"What?" I yelled into it without bothering to check the caller.

"Morning, sunshine," Weston said cheerfully.

"Screw you." I hung up and tossed the phone onto the floor.

I didn't have the patience for his lecture bullshit this early.

I finally managed to drag my hungover ass into the shower an hour later. I kept myself level against the wall, granting the water permission to sprinkle down my body, and my mind went over yesterday's events.

I wanted to erase the day from ever happening. Flashbacks came back faster than the drops scattering down my naked body.

Weston had believed me about my rape. My father had talked about my mom. My arm went to the shower wall, and I took a deep breath. The shots of vodka. More shots of vodka. I couldn't stand up straight. I'd called Weston. My body stiffened.

Dear God, I called Weston.

My brain scrambled, trying its hardest to recollect every-thing I'd said, and it hit me.

Shoot. I'd told him I'd been fingering myself to thoughts of him screwing me.

Vodka is one chatty bitch.

Then, he'd basically told me he'd been doing the same thing, and we got each other off. Everything I'd done in my bed last night came back to me. I thought about Weston's dirty words and how easily he had gotten me off.

I captured one of my breasts, playing with my hard nipple. I envisioned Weston behind me, pressing me against the glass wall with his voice in my ear as the shower drowned out our moans. My hand roamed down my thigh, and I plunged a finger inside myself. I repeated the same motions Weston had instructed me to do over the phone. I slid one finger in, then out, and then pushed another one in.

My hazy, hungover brain couldn't remember how I'd gotten so drunk, but it remembered everything I'd done with the man I shouldn't have been having phone sex with.

sixteen

ELISE

Weston wasn't in the office when I walked in.

But Wendy was.

I gulped, and my heart did a nosedive at his absence.

Was his call this morning to bail?

"Oh, hey. We haven't officially met. I'm Wendy," she greeted when she saw me. "Wes called. He's running a few minutes late and asked me to relay the message to you."

Wes called.

I wanted to roll my eyes at her nickname for him.

She watched me as I walked over to the couch and sat down with my purse resting in my lap.

"Thanks," I said, bouncing a knee.

She pulled herself up from the chair, walked around the desk, and leaned against it. "How do you two know each other?" Her head cocked to the side.

I tugged on my lower lip with my teeth as I tried to figure out the answer to her question.

Did Weston tell her a story, and she is testing me to see if it matches up with mine? I wasn't sure what her motive was.

She waved her hand through the air when she noticed my hesitation. "It's personal—I get it. I apologize if I seem intrusive, but you can't blame a woman for being curious."

Actually, I could.

"Curious about what?" I asked coldly.

If there was one thing I hated, it was nosy people. Problem was, I couldn't piss her off too bad. We needed her office for our meetings.

"I promise I only have good intentions," she said cautiously. "I don't understand why he's seeing you in secret. It's not like him. He's always been a by-the-book kind of guy." She laughed, tilting her head back. "You should've seen him in college. It was hell, trying to pry him away from his studies and drag him out to have fun."

I cracked a small smile. "That doesn't surprise me. I'm sure nothing has changed." Well, other than the fact that he had stroked his cock to my voice last night.

"But he's different with you. When you leave, I talk to him and can tell there's something. He's getting attached to you. I knew he had an interest in you, but now, it's more than that. You're something to him, and I haven't decided if it's healthy or not." She paused, like she was debating whether to elaborate. "What are you to him? Who is he to you?"

I stayed silent, pulled my phone from my purse, and checked to see if I had any texts from him.

What is Weston to me? What am I to Weston? I didn't know the answers to those questions and was terrified to find them out.

"He cares about you," she pointed out again, not letting me off the hook.

"He cares about all his patients," I threw back, scowling at her and then moving my attention to the door.

Weston needed to hurry his ass up before I snapped on this woman to stop her prying questions. I knew she probably had Weston's best interests at heart, but I didn't want to hear her say he was making a mistake with me.

"That's true, but he *really* cares for you. Trust me, it's not a patient type of care. It's different. It's something more, so please don't hurt him. He's a good man."

The scowl on my face morphed into fear. She was right. I hurt everyone around me. I was afraid I'd do the same to him.

"Sorry I'm late," Weston said, barging into the room, and Wendy's mouth slammed shut. His attention swung back and forth between Wendy and me. "Everything okay?"

Wendy smacked her hands against her knees and smiled at him brightly. "Just having some girl talk."

I shrugged when his gaze moved to me.

"Okay," he drew out.

"I'll leave you two to it," Wendy said. She started to walk out of the room but stopped to give him a quick kiss on the cheek before shutting the door and leaving.

Wowza.

Screw Wendy.

I wasn't sure if the woman was for me or against me.

Weston threw his bag on the desk before shrugging out of his coat. His eyes were tired and his face unshaven.

"Hey," I said when he turned to me. I crossed my legs and waved shyly at him. *When the hell did I become shy?*

"Hey there," he said, upbeat and chirpy.

His attitude didn't match his behavior. He grabbed the chair behind the desk and wheeled it in front of me—like always— but he did it quietly this time without food in his hand.

Yep. Hello, Mr. Awkward.

I'd told him it wouldn't be that way, but it was like any other one-night stand. You couldn't wait to get the person naked, not thinking about future consequences, only the urge between your legs. If you knew the other person, you swore it wouldn't change anything with your relationship, but no matter what, it did. You either had to sneak out of their house early in the morning and pretend it hadn't happened or face the painful morning after. Even if it had just been phone sex, it had changed us.

"We're not going to make this weird, okay?" he said, making himself comfortable while I slipped out of my jacket.

"So, you've known Wendy for a while?" I asked curiously, wanting to change the subject. Wendy sounded like a safe topic.

He nodded. "I have."

"How do you two know each other?"

He bent back, grabbed a water bottle from his bag, and took a giant gulp. "We used to date." He averted his eyes to the floor and took another drink.

I could see it. He and Wendy fitted each other. They were both smart, successful, and rational. She was gorgeous and most likely someone Weston would end up settling down with. Wendy was also the opposite of me.

"Why did you guys break up?" I pushed.

He shrugged in disinterest. "We grew apart, I guess. We're better off as friends."

"Oh," I said, the word popping out of my mouth.

I wanted to press him for more, but at the same time, the jealous monster inside me didn't want to hear him talking about being with another woman. I didn't want to think about Weston pleasuring her like he had me.

"We need to address the elephant in the room." His face turned serious. "I don't want this to be weird."

I mulled over whether to play coy. Maybe if I acted like I had no idea what he was talking about, he'd think he'd imagined it. No, unlike my other guys, Weston was smarter than that.

"Bringing it up makes it weird," I pointed out.

"What happened last night should've never happened."

"I know. I'm sorry." My eyes went to my lap as I fidgeted with the strap of my bag.

"Look at me," he insisted ruggedly.

I peeked up, my eyes hitting his.

"Don't you dare apologize. This isn't your fault. You were drunk, and I should've never played along. But I did, and that's on me. I abused my position, and it won't happen again. I want you to know I'm sorry. I didn't want to stand you up today, but after careful consideration, I think this should be our last session."

His words kicked me in the chest.

"What? No. Absolutely not."

"What we did was wrong. I have a certain code of conduct I have to abide by and"--he lowered his voice--"getting you off is certainly against it. You're a victim of sexual abuse. I should've never taken it that far with you. I took advantage of you, and I'm sorry."

We never broke eye contact.

"You took advantage of me?" I hissed. "You can't be serious?"

He didn't answer me.

"To hell with your code of conduct. We did nothing wrong. I'm not paying you to do anything for me. I'm not your client, and you didn't take advantage of me." I tried to keep my voice low, but every word grew louder. I thrusted my finger in his direction. "You gave me something I needed. *You* made me feel like I wasn't a victim. *You* let me forget about everything that had happened to me. *You* helped me. Whether or not you want to believe it, you did."

We'd done nothing wrong. We were two consenting adults who had wanted to talk dirty to each other. That wasn't against any rules.

"I understand how you feel, but—"

My hand shot forward, stopping him. "I won't talk to anyone else but you. You're the only person I feel comfortable with. You're the only person I'll confide in."

I threw up my hands, tears pricking at my eyes. I didn't want to get emotional, but the thought of him leaving me was just too much. I'd only been around him a short time, but I was getting attached. I anticipated seeing him each meeting. It was the highlight of my day.

"You believe me," I croaked. "Do you know how long I've been waiting for that? Do you know how long I've waited for someone to be Team Elise? You did that, and I'll be damned if you think I'm going to let you go without a fight. We won't have phone sex again. That was a one-time thing. But you will keep seeing me. Now, shut up and forget about last night, and let's talk."

He grinned. "All right then, Miss Bossy Pants. I'm here to stay."

"Damn straight," I replied, returning his smile.

All the tension in the room burned away.

"I think we left off after the guy came into your room and forced himself on you," he said, getting straight to business.

"Well, shit. You go from leaving me to this? No warm-ups?"

"I stay, and you give me what I want." He stopped, his choice of words hitting him. "Wow, that didn't sound right."

I laughed. "I know what you meant. Get your mind out of the gutter, Doctor, and get over what happened with us."

I was trying to convince myself to do the same thing. The ridiculous fantasy I had of Weston being with me was unrealistic. That could never happen. The quicker I realized that, the better.

"All day yesterday and all night, I fought with myself, wanting to know everything you'd been through." His eyes darkened in agony. "I wish I could've been there to save you. There were other men, right?"

I folded my hands in my lap, and my body warmed. "Yes."

His face was red, angry, but he was trying to hold in his anger for me. "Do you know how many?"

"Seven," I told him quickly. I had the number down.

His brows furrowed together, causing his glasses to fall down his nose. "Seven different men have raped you?"

"Yes," I answered, a dirty taste hitting my tongue.

"And how many men have you been sexually active with?"

"Twenty-two," I answered in shame, waiting for the look of disgust to cross his face. I'd had more men inside of me than years I'd been alive.

"Is that counting the rapes or willingly?"

"Counting the rapes and the men I had sex with because my father had forced me to go on dates with them, plus the random guys I've screwed. All of them."

I didn't want to count the rapes, but I did. It was embarrassing, revealing that number to him, but I hadn't wanted to lie. He'd stayed to help me. I needed to be honest. But he didn't flinch at my number. He just stared at me with sorrow in his eyes. I wasn't sure which one was worse—pity or disgust.

"Did you know any of the men who raped you?" Like with his anger, he tried to keep his voice steady, but with each word, it was growing harder for him.

"No." My mouth turned dry. "I've seen a few around the city and at business dinners with my father, but I never knew them personally. It normally happened before he started doing business with them."

Want a business deal? Have my daughter in exchange. That was basically my father's company motto.

"And Peter? Was he part of the business deal at first?"

I shook my head. "No, which is probably what made my father the angriest. He received no benefit in exchange for me sleeping with Peter. So, when my father found out Peter had gone to the police, my father knew his ass was on the line. So, he made sure to shut Peter up and sent me to Sun Gate. He told them that I was abusing narcotics, sleeping with older men, and now that my lover was behind bars, I was getting back at my father by accusing him of allowing men to rape me. So, when I told my first psychologist, she went to the board. They revisited the issue with my father, he lied and most likely cut Sun Gate a large check to ignore what I'd said. According to him and everyone else, I do all this for attention."

"I want to kill him," Weston hissed.

"Welcome to my world."

seventeen

ELISE

"What are you doing here?" I asked my father, shutting my front door in hesitation at the sight of him in my apartment.

He was slumped against the couch cushions with a glass of amber liquor in his hand. My lips screwed into a grimace while he stared at me with bloodshot eyes from across the room. I looked away from him, noticing the empty bottle of scotch on the table with the cap next to it.

"I wanted to visit my baby girl," he slurred, patting the seat next to him. He held up the glass in a cheers motion, turned it up to his lips, and took a long pull.

Just great. He was wasted—the last thing I needed to deal with.

"You're drunk." I unbuckled my coat and placed it on the hook, my stomach twisting with disgust. I wanted to turn around, leave, and not come back until he was gone.

Unfortunately, it was too late to do that, so I needed to convince him to leave.

He held his hands up in the air, his smile turning sinister. "Guilty."

"Then, why don't you go home and sober up?"

Him being here was a bad idea. He was an angry and emotional drunk—the worst kind.

He polished off his drink, slammed it on the table, and then struggled to stand. "I need a favor." It took him a moment to gain composure of himself before he loosened his tie and came my way.

My shoulders grew tight, and I crossed my arms across my chest. "What kind of favor?" Favors for him were never good.

"I have a potential client flying in from France," he said, stopping only a few feet from me and settling his hands on the dining room table. "He's big time, high powered, and reputable to be in business with. You know how much wealthy men appreciate an attractive woman. I need you to entertain him for a few hours, possibly a night—whatever he prefers. He wants a date for dinner, and I'd like you to show him around the city. It would do you good to get out as well. You're always complaining about being bored, sitting around this place." He grinned wide like he'd conjured up the perfect plan with his deranged mind.

I gulped before having the ability to speak. "Hire a whore."

"Have you seen the whores around this city? They're trashy. They're disgusting," he said, scoffing in disgust. "Every decent one got busted in that ridiculous prostitution raid. I can't send him a ragged piece-of-shit hooker that could be picked up on any corner. He needs someone beautiful. He needs high class, and that's what you're going to give him."

The hell I am. "Did you just refer to me, your daughter, as a hooker?"

He moved his jaw back and forth before clenching it tight. "I don't ask you for much."

Is he kidding?

"Nuh-uh, I'm not doing it," I said, throwing my hands up. "I thought this was over!"

"Just one last time, and I promise, no more."

"Absolutely not. I've allowed you to take advantage of me for far too long."

My chest ached. I knew deep down that there was no way I was getting out of it.

When he wanted something, he got it.

"It's not happening," I continued to argue, swallowing a large lump forming in the base of my throat. I shook my head violently and stalked toward my bedroom. "Now, go home and sleep off all that alcohol. You reek."

When his fist pounded against the table, I jumped and whipped around. His venomous, cold eyes sparked to life as he charged my way, pushing me back before I had the chance to flee. I landed with a loud thud against the wall and gasped when I felt his large body hover over mine.

"You will do this," he snarled.

Every limb in my body shook as he manhandled me in the corner. He'd revamped from extremely intoxicated to highly alert in seconds.

"Let's think of this as your job. It's not like I don't pay you for these favors." His face leveled with mine.

I shook my head, cringing when the smell of alcohol hit my nostrils.

"You've wanted a car. Let's see this as a simple exchange, shall we?" His spit splattered against my cheeks.

"No," I argued, glancing away from him as I tried to calm my breathing. "I'm not selling my body for a car."

He bared his teeth, his nostrils flaring. Nobody told this man no, especially not me.

"You'll do it."

I gasped when his body pushed into mine roughly. "The hell I will!"

"Don't make me force you. You know neither of us will enjoy that."

I shut my eyes, taking three long breaths before opening them up. I stared up at him, his face still wrapped up in fury, and I knew having this conversation with him in this state was a horrible idea.

"I'll think about it," I said, forcing my voice to stay calm. "Go home, and we'll talk about this in the morning."

I attempted to duck underneath his arm to maneuver around him but didn't make it too far. I shrieked out in pain when his hand forcefully wrapped around my arm and he threw me back against the wall.

He pinned me against it, his arms cornering me in, and grabbed both of my hands to stretch them above my head. I cried out when he pressed down on them painfully so I couldn't move. His lips curled up while I struggled to break free.

"You're just like her, you know that, you cunt? At least she was smart enough to spread her legs for something of value. But you do it for free, *whore*."

I ignored him, squirming for release. My legs shook while I tried to fight against him, which only made him angrier. More pain shot through me as his hold tightened. I whimpered as he glared at me with amusement, and terror immediately hit me.

This was it. He'd been angry with me before, but this time was different. His eyes had always been full of hate and anger, but they were twisted with something darker tonight. Something evil.

"Whores don't deserve respect," he said, lowering his voice to a whisper. "If you don't respect yourself or your body, you deserve pain."

I shut my eyes, the scent of alcohol growing stronger.

"You look just like her, just like that stupid slut. God cursed you by giving you her attractiveness. He fucked you right from the very start."

A gasp of air escaped my chest when he released an arm, but my stomach coiled when I realized he wasn't letting me go. No, he was just getting started. He traced the outline of my mouth with cold, fumbling fingers before sliding them down between my breastbone, my stomach, and then to my waist.

"God, I miss her so much," he muttered.

I shuddered when his mouth hit my ear. My heart pounded so hard against my chest that I was sure it would crack open my rib cage and fall at our feet. My bones wanted to shake themselves out of my skin and flee the scene.

This wasn't happening. *No.* This couldn't be happening right now.

"Father ... stop," I said, holding back a scream. My breathing constricted, my heart beating against my lungs, but I tried to do my best to act normal.

"God, I wanted her so much. I miss her. I miss her touch."

I began to panic when he balled up my shirt in his fist, his clammy hand roaming along the bare skin of my stomach. My skin crawled at his touch.

I bit my lip when his erection pressed between my thighs.

Why aren't I screaming? Fighting? Why can't I move?

I felt paralyzed.

"She loved it when I fucked her." He thrust into me again, rougher this time. "But eventually, that wasn't enough. I wish she were here now, so I could show her how a real man fucks. Do *you* know how a real man fucks? Not one who's paying for it?"

I shrank back at the feel of his tongue darting along my earlobe while his hand slid between my legs.

It wasn't the first time something like this had happened.

When my father drank, he got mean. He also got nostalgic. He missed my mom, and all the bad shit came back up with every sip of alcohol. His mind would go into a different world, and he'd think I was her—but after a few minutes, he'd wake up and snap back into reality. He'd never let it get this far before. I was terrified to find out where his limits were tonight. As each day passed, he became more and more of a monster.

Panic engulfed me the moment he unsnapped the button of my jeans. I tried to swat his hand away, but he slammed me harder against the wall.

"Don't you dare fight it, or it'll turn ugly. I'm going to get you prepared for this guy tomorrow. You will meet him, and you will do whatever he wants."

"Father!" I finally managed to scream out, trying to push him away again.

"I've been waiting to have you in my arms again," he muttered, his mouth back to my ear, his fingers fidgeting with my zipper.

"I'm not her!" I struggled to bring up a knee, aiming it toward his groin, but his hold on me was too strong.

He continued to grind against me, his hand dipping into my pants while I scratched at him. I used my nails, teeth, anything to move, but he wasn't letting go.

His hand went to my mouth, blocking my voice as I screamed for help. He cursed when I managed to sink my teeth into the rough skin of his palm, and he brought his hand back to inspect the wound before slapping me across the face.

As my head whiplashed to the side, it dawned on me—I was about to be raped by my father. This wasn't a strange man I'd never met. This was the one who was supposed to love and protect me. I pushed to breathe, working hard for it, but I lost all my power and will to fight. My head fell back at another smack in the face. I drifted into another world, to the place I went to every time this happened to me, my real-life nightmare.

Another smack woke me from my trance, and I screamed for help again. My head flew forward, knocking into his, at the sound of the door opening. My eyes shot open to see Marlon barreling into the room. When he took in the scene of us, his entire body stopped, suspended, like he was frozen in time.

I peeked over my father's shoulder at Marlon with pleading eyes when I heard the quiet zip of my father's pants through the silence.

Marlon stared in shock, and I mouthed, *"Please do something!"*

My father was oblivious to Marlon's presence as he harshly pulled down on the waist of my jeans. I didn't know what Marlon would do, but I could tell he was contemplating with himself. If he stood up for me, he'd be fired and unable to support his family.

"Holy shit!" Marlon finally yelled, his face reddening as he rushed toward us.

"Help me!" I gasped.

He grabbed my father's arm. "Mr. Parks!" he screamed, tugging him back.

My father ignored him, his attention focused on attempting to get my pants off.

"Mr. Parks!" Marlon yelled again, louder this time, but he got nothing.

I hovered forward when the weight of his body left me, and Marlon slammed him onto the floor.

"What the hell?!" my father yelled, glaring at Marlon.

"Go to your room and lock the door," Marlon instructed me, pushing my father back down when he tried to get up and make a grab for me.

"Elise!" my father screamed, his arm reaching out, his face

falling. "What did I do?" he asked, his voice breaking as reality sank in.

I ignored him, nearly tripping when I grabbed my purse and sprinted to my bedroom. I twisted the lock, double-checking it was secure, and tears began to pour down my face. I tossed my purse onto my bed and began rummaging through it until I found my phone. I had to get out of this place.

I called the one person I knew would help me.

Him.

He'd become my go-to.

This man I hardly knew was becoming my savior.

"I need you," I cried out when he picked up. I tried to sound controlled, but I knew the warning was clear.

"What's going on?" Weston asked.

"I need you right now. Please, come get me." I ran my arm along my face to rid it of the tears I wished I weren't crying.

"I'm on my way."

"Meet me in the back entrance by the fire escape."

"Got it."

Just like that. No questions asked, just, "I'm on my way."

Those four words meant more to me than any dollar in the world. My entire life, I'd been surrounded by people who only saw me as an opportunity or a slut. But Weston, he saw more than that. He wasn't there for me to get something in return. He was there for me simply because he cared.

I hurriedly tossed clothes into my bag, pulled my jeans back up, and buckled them before throwing a sweatshirt over my head and pulling up the hood. I flung the bag over my shoulder and opened my bedroom door. The room was quiet and empty. I didn't know where my father or Marlon had gone, but I wasn't going to wait around to find out.

I ran out of my apartment, down the hallway, pushed open the emergency exit door, and sprinted down the stairs. I'd been sneaking out of the complex for fourteen years. I knew the building like the back of my hand.

I hit the bottom floor, my breathing labored, and dashed into the back alley. I scanned it from side to side.

Weston isn't here yet.

I sank back against the building, hiding in the shadows next to a dumpster so I could be invisible. My father would be searching for me.

I tapped my foot against the pavement while I waited for whoever would find me first. I froze when I heard the creaky door swing open, followed by footsteps approaching me.

I swallowed hard in terror.

Weston was too late.

eighteen

ELISE

My knees buckled as the footsteps grew closer. I crept behind the dumpster, my heart racing harder and harder.

My father won't look behind it, right?

He wouldn't think I'd resort to hiding behind something so disgusting.

I shrieked when a man's boots came into view, his head popping up in front of me.

"Just lettin' you know, there ain't any good shit in there," he said, tossing a trash bag into the dumpster. "But it's all yours."

I ignored him, and he smacked the dumpster lid a few times before turning around and leaving. I peeped to the side and noticed bright lights heading down the alley. I blinked a few times, trying to make out the car, and jumped into the alleyway. I rushed over, swung open the door, and hopped in quickly.

"Go!" I shrieked. "Just go!" I slammed the door shut.

Weston eyeballed me in concern.

I smacked the glove compartment in frustration. "Gun it, goddammit!"

He geared the car in drive, stomped on the gas pedal, and we shot forward. I buckled my seat belt while he picked up speed, turning onto the street. I threw my bag in the backseat and then took a deep, relaxing breath that did anything but relax me. My blood was still boiling, my pulse still sky high, and I was on the brink of losing it. My head fell sideways against the chilly window while I prayed for God to erase the night's events from my brain.

A few miles passed before he silenced the radio.

"Where to?" he asked.

"Anywhere but there," I answered, my breath forming a circle against the glass. I didn't care where he took me as long as it wasn't home. I was never going back there.

He nodded, and I didn't question where we were going. I only shut my eyes and stayed silent—apart from the uncontrolled sobs tearing through my body. When he pulled into the parking garage, I dragged my head away from the window, and he cut the engine.

"Is this okay?" he asked, observing me and unbuckling his seat belt.

I nodded. It was more than okay.

He leaned into the backseat, grabbed my bag, and got out of the car. I pulled myself up to find him waiting for me. His shoulders slumped down when he saw me in the light.

"Not again," he said, dragging his hands through his hair. "Motherfucker!" His tennis shoes slammed against the concrete, his mouth biting into his fist.

I hadn't looked in the mirror in my race to get out of there, but I knew I had a few battle wounds from my fight. I'd been beaten up *again*, stranded *again*, and I was still fighting the tears back when he took my hand in his. He walked me up the stairwell and up to his apartment. I knew, eventually, he'd grow tired of playing the savior and quit answering my calls.

"I'm going to grab something for your face," he said, turning on the lights when we reached his apartment. "Get comfortable on the couch."

I slipped off my shoes and followed his instructions while he went into the kitchen.

"This time, you'd better tell me what happened," he said, kneeling in front of me and sweeping my hood back to get a better view.

I winced when a crisp bag of frozen veggies slid across my face and landed on my cheek. He captured my tears with a single finger while staring at me, waiting.

"He was drunk," I said, as if that should explain everything.

He waited for me to elaborate, but I only sat there and hung my head in shame. I didn't want him to know. I was embarrassed. It was humiliating that my life and my family was this dysfunctional. I was ashamed I hadn't had the strength to fight him off. I'd done nothing. I'd stood there, frozen to the wall, and allowed him to do whatever he wanted. I was a coward.

"Was it your father?" he asked impatiently. "Is he the one who did this?"

"Yes." I moved the bag away from my stinging cheek, replacing it with my palm.

"Tell me what happened, please," he said, his hand squeezing my leg.

"I don't want to talk about it."

He groaned, moving his hand from my leg up to my chin. "I'm not playing this game again."

I wished I'd respected myself enough to get away from my father long ago.

"It's not a game. I just don't feel like being judged right now," I snapped, taking my animosity out on the last person who should've been on the receiving end. I was lashing out at the person who had helped me, but I couldn't help it. I didn't want to answer his questions. I didn't want to say those words.

He groaned, throwing his head back. "Why do you always say that? You know I'm not judging you. You know I never have. So, stop trying to use that as a cop-out."

"Oh, yeah, right," I muttered. "You might act like you don't, but there's no way you don't think what everyone else does. There's no way you can't think I'm just this stupid slut asking for this to keep happening to her."

"I don't think you deserve anything that's happened to you, and I certainly don't think you deserve to be sitting on my couch, beaten up for the second time. It has to stop, but that's not going to happen if you keep sitting here, silent."

"Not tonight." I got up from the couch, moved away from him, and headed into the kitchen. I opened the fridge and snatched a bottle of wine. I needed something to drown my thoughts out.

I turned around to grab a glass and shrieked when I bumped into something hard. I glanced up, my chin hitting his chest as he held out his hand, his eyes staring down at me.

"Fine," I groaned, handing over the bottle.

He plucked it from my hold and tossed it into the trash can.

"That's wasting perfectly good wine," I argued, throwing my hand toward the discarded bottle.

"And? I don't care."

I turned back to the fridge to grab a bottle of water. "I'm not talking about it tonight, so give it up."

I didn't have the energy to deal with Dr. Snyder at the moment. I wanted the Weston who knew how to shut it and let things go for a minute.

He rocked back on his heels. "I understand. No questions tonight. But there will be questions tomorrow."

I nodded. I'd find a way to get out of it then too.

"There are clean sheets on your bed."

My bed. I wasn't sure if he'd caught onto his words, but I had.

"You can stay here as long as you'd like," he added.

I knew I couldn't stay with Weston forever. But he'd give me enough time to come up with a plan. I could get a job and save up for my own place.

I stared at his chest muscles showing through the thin white T-shirt while he rested his back against the counter.

"Is there anything you need?" he asked.

I shook my head, playing with the bottle in my hand. "I'm good." I was still in shock, but now that I was away from my father, I was beginning to feel better.

He flipped off the light when we left the kitchen. "Let me know if you do."

"Do you ..." I hesitated, unsure if I had the guts to ask. "Do you think I can sleep in your bed tonight?"

"That's not a good idea."

"I understand." I was unable to meet his eyes.

He'd help me, but it wouldn't go any further.

"That bed is pretty comfy. You'll fall asleep as soon as you hit the sheets," he said, attempting to make me feel better at his rejection.

I nodded while walking toward the bedroom.

He grabbed my hand in his, leading me into the room. "Sleep tight," he whispered, squeezing my hand before releasing it and shutting the door.

I slipped out of my clothes, leaving just a tank top and panties on, and climbed into bed.

The tears started as soon as I turned the lamp off. I wondered what my father was thinking—what he was doing and if he felt guilty for what he'd done. I also wondered if he already had a plan to get me back for leaving.

"I hate him," I whispered into my tear-soaked pillowcase.

I cried. I cried for what seemed like hours. I had a good, long, and overdue cry.

I jumped when my door opened, and a dark figure stalked toward the bed. I shrieked as their arms wrapped around my body, pulled me out of bed, and I tried to fight them off.

"Shh," the gentle voice said. "It's just me."

My body settled, and my head fell into the crook of Weston's shoulder as I allowed him to carry me to his bedroom. He laid me down gently and pulled the covers over me.

"To hell with good ideas," he growled, snuggling up behind me.

His lips kissed my ear, and I relaxed in his warm arms while the beat of his heart soothed me to sleep.

nineteen

ELISE

Goose bumps collided against my skin as I pulled up the blanket until it smacked into my chin. I sprawled out my legs across the crisp sheets and scanned the room.

I was in Weston's bedroom.

In his bed.

I was in my hot-as-hell and completely off-limits shrink's bed. I couldn't stop myself from getting into these bizarre situations. My life kept getting weirder and weirder.

I stared at the ceiling and blew out a breath. Warmth replaced the goose bumps when I realized how comfortable I was there. It was like his bed was where I belonged.

I lifted to look around the room better. It was large. The king-size bed took up most of the space. A big-screen TV hung directly across from me and over a dresser covered with framed photos and bottles of cologne.

I slumped back down, my mind running at full speed.

What time was it? How long had I been sleeping?

Fear pulsated through my veins as I wondered what was in store for me.

My father would find me. I had no doubts. He'd be out, scouring the streets, until he had me back. He'd kill me or anyone else before he let me out of his grasp.

So, my new goal was to disappear. I had some cash in my bag, and I was sure Weston would help me. I needed to start a new life, get a new identity, one where I wouldn't be sold out for business deals. I wanted freedom. I was in the driver's seat now. I was in control—at least, that was what I wanted to think.

I scrubbed at my arm, feeling the tenderness from where my father's hands had been last night. I wanted to erase his touch, to trick my mind that it'd never happened. I tried to convince myself he would've stopped, but I knew better. The expression on his face had told me there was no stopping him.

He'd wanted to hurt me—to transfer the pain eating at him. It's what he'd been doing my entire life. He hungered to scar me the same way my mother had him. He took his resentment for her out on me because I was her living replica. I'd always be a memory of what he'd lost and what she'd put him through.

The bed sank when I slammed my arms down to my sides.

"I hate him!" I screeched.

I knotted my fists into tiny balls, swinging them back and forth on the bed before grabbing the first thing I could get my hands on. Anger coursed through me as I hurled a pillow across the room, and it smacked against the wall. I shook my head, kicked my feet, and my lungs fired up as I screamed at the ceiling.

He was destroying me. No, he'd already destroyed me and wasn't done yet. He wanted to massacre me. He wanted to crush me into small, helpless pieces and laugh in my face. He wanted to drain every drop of sanity and fight I had left. He was going to eradicate me until he felt vindicated.

I kicked my legs, darkness flooding my eyesight, and gripped the sheets. My mind tormented me. Visions of my life swirled through my head, putting my struggles on full display. The men, the ones who'd raped me, were so clear. My father's vicious words swept through next, followed by the abuse and his indecent embraces. I was done crying. I was finished fighting. I wanted it all to go away.

"Calm down," a soft voice whispered into my ear. "You have to calm down for me."

My feet stopped, and my body went slack. I rested my head on the pillow and opened one eye at a time. I struggled to speak as I eyed Weston above me. He'd heard me.

I wouldn't be surprised if his neighbors had heard me.

He cautiously reached out and waited for my reaction before caressing my forehead. "No one is going to hurt you anymore, okay? I'm here. I will protect you."

My breathing shuddered, coming out in tiny pants, while my body came down from my rage. His voice and touch instantly soothed me, evaporating the darkness.

"Good morning," he said, his fingers brushing circles across my skin. He bent his head down to my ear. "I made eggs. They're organic."

I gave him a weird look. "Organic? Is that your plan for breaking the awkwardness?"

He grinned. "Yes, ma'am. Food always makes problems go away. And they're not full of hormones and chemicals, making it even better."

"Always the responsible one," I muttered. "I'm not sure how we went from me having a nervous breakdown to eggs, but I'll take it."

"Well, I figured you'd want a full belly before I began my interrogation."

I pulled away from him to lift myself onto my knees and pushed my hair back. "I'm surprised you're not kicking me out of your place for the scene I just made."

He shrugged. "I'd be more concerned if you didn't let it all out."

"What? You seriously can't think that's normal."

"For someone with that much hurt and anger built up, yes. That's exactly what you needed. It's good to have a freak-out sometimes." He held out his hand. "Now, let's eat."

I slipped my hand into his, allowing him to pull me up from the bed, and kept my gaze on his back while following him into the kitchen. I could make out his shoulder muscles through his shirt, and a pair of black athletic shorts fell loose around his waist.

"I like this look," I said, pulling out a stool and watching him move around me to the stove.

"Huh?" he asked.

I gestured to his clothes. "This look. You, tired, just waking up in the morning."

He tugged at the hem of his T-shirt. "Thanks." He pulled a spatula from a drawer and began piling eggs on two plates. "I wasn't sure what your breakfast of choice was or how you liked your eggs, so I went with scrambled again. Everyone loves scrambled eggs." He sprinkled some pepper on them before adding bacon and a slice of toast.

I leaned back in the chair. "That's fine. I honestly don't have that much of an appetite."

"Too bad." He handed me the plate. "You're eating."

My eyes bulged at the heaping portions. "I could live on that for a week."

I wasn't a healthy eater. I didn't have three to five meals a day and didn't eat enough fruits and veggies. I ate when I felt like it, usually ice cream, sandwiches, or whatever takeout was delivered.

"Eat," he demanded.

I groaned, snatching a piece of bacon. I took a giant bite at the same time he set a glass of orange juice in front of me. "So, where do we go from here?"

"I'll be gone for a while today." Guilt was evident on his face. He felt bad for leaving me. "They found a replacement for me at Sun Gate. I need to go there and clear out my things."

I perked up in my chair. "Can I go?"

He paused mid-drink and gaped at me.

"It would be nice to take a drive and clear my head. I need to get away from this place even if it's only for a while."

He pointed his cup my way and smiled. "Sure. I could use some good company."

I grinned.

"Finish eating, and then we'll head out."

"You'd better give me a good time, Counselor," I said, taking a giant bite.

He chuckled. "I'll try my hardest."

twenty

ELISE

I fiddled with the radio knob and changed the station every five seconds until I found a tolerable song while I waited for Weston.

I hadn't wanted to look up when he pulled into Sun Gate's parking lot. But like a car crash, I couldn't help myself. I blinked a few times before focusing on the normal-appearing building. Nothing had changed, but that still hadn't stopped me from flipping it the bird.

Weston was gone less than ten minutes before he came strolling back through the parking lot with a cardboard box balanced in his hands. He casually walked toward the car, snow crunching underneath his boots, while the wind smacked him in the face. He paused for a second, hiked his knee up to rest the box on it, and pushed his glasses further up his nose.

God, the man was adorable. He was handsome. He was nice. He had so many good qualities that it was overwhelming.

I couldn't believe I was referring to a man as adorable or handsome. I tended not to refer to men as either one of those things. My terms of endearments tended to be along the lines of *sexy, hot as fuck, fuckable*. Never adorable or handsome.

Then again, I'd never met a guy like Weston. My *hot as fuck* men were typically womanizers who only wanted a girlfriend while they were getting their dick sucked. As soon as they exploded in your mouth, they had a change of heart and didn't want to be tied down.

"I see this place seems just as lovely as it did three years ago," I joked after he set the box in the backseat and got back into the car.

"Hey now, look on the bright side of things. If you hadn't been here, we would've never met. We wouldn't be here, sitting in my car after enjoying a mini road trip."

He had a point there. The place had never hurt me. It had taken me away from my prison. And most importantly, it'd brought Weston to me.

He tapped my knee. "Now, lunch. I'm starving."

Because of the snow, the streets were deserted while we drove to get food. We ordered through the drive-through but didn't eat until he pulled onto the side of a vacant road a few miles out of town. He shifted the car in park but left it running.

"I used to come here and think," he said before opening the food bag. "I can't even count the number of times I ate my lunch in this spot."

My stomach embarrassingly growled at the smell of greasy French fries, and I peered out the window to the small park. "I don't blame you."

It was the most serene place I'd ever seen. A partially frozen, narrow creek flowed between rows of trees. Patches of melted snow and ice covered sections of the dying grass. Quiet tranquility surrounded the entire place. There were no people there. There were no tables. The only feature other than nature's mark was a small wooden bench in front of the creek.

Weston handed me a cheeseburger and situated a container of fries against the shifter until it stood up without falling. I took a large bite and then a sip of Coke.

"Aren't you going to eat?" I asked.

The burger in his lap remained untouched.

He shook his head, his mood changing. "Will you please tell me what happened last night?"

"Why don't we eat first?"

He unwrapped his burger and took a giant bite. His lunch was gone in three bites. He was on a mission. I continued to nibble on my burger to buy me some extra time.

"It's bad," I finally said.

I wasn't sure how many more awful experiences I could endure before I completely lost it. I was raped several times. I'd overdosed on pills on more than one occasion. My father had sexually assaulted me. I didn't want to keep feeling sorry for myself. I didn't want to keep thinking about it. All my life, I'd thought it was wrong to tell somebody what had happened. I'd been told that telling my story was begging for attention.

"Look at me," he demanded, and my gaze shot over to him. "You're one of the strongest people I know. I don't know how the hell you do it, but you do."

"Do what?"

"Stay strong. Do you know how many people would've given up by now? But you keep going. You're strong, but I need you to do me a favor. Please take that strength you have in you and tell me what happened. Release some of that burden off you. You need to get it out."

"He tried to rape me."

He nodded, as if he'd already known the answer, and squeezed his eyes shut.

I jumped at the sound of the horn blasting when his fist connected with the steering wheel.

"I want to kill him!" he screamed, and another roar came from the horn. He threw his door open, jumped out of the car, and stalked away from me. He cursed to the sky, kicking rocks while he moved toward the stream.

I reached over the console to turn off the ignition before going after him. I found him slumped down on the wooden bench with his head hanging between his open legs.

"Hey," I said softly, standing in front of him, tucking my hands into my sweatshirt pocket.

"Get back in the car," he insisted without raising his head. "It's freezing out here."

"I'm not going back until you do."

"Please," he begged. "Get back in the car. I need a minute to clear my head."

I brushed a layer of snow from the bench before plopping down next to him. I scooted closer until my thighs met his and rested my head against his drooping shoulder.

"Marlon, one of his employees, heard me screaming and stopped him," I said, trying to calm Weston.

He lifted his head and turned to face me. That was when I noticed his eyes were watery.

"Thank God," he said, exhaling a breath. "Now, please get in the car. Just give me five minutes. *Please.*"

"Okay, but if you're not back in five minutes, I'm coming back out here."

He responded with a nod and then bowed his head.

I turned the heat on high when I got back into the car and watched him through the window. He was torn. Regretful. My confession had made him as broken as I was.

"Is everything okay?" I asked when he returned.

"Yeah. I just needed a minute to think."

"Please don't be upset with yourself. You couldn't have stopped anything."

"I should've been there for you," he muttered. His eyes were red and cheeks wind burned.

"Don't you dare beat yourself up about this, okay? You've helped me more than I could have ever asked for." I needed to lighten the mood. I'd told him what had happened, but it was over, and I wanted to forget about it. "Can I drive?"

His chin lifted as he stared at me, trying to figure out if I was being serious or not. "Do you have your driver's license?"

"No."

"Then, no."

"Come on. I'm twenty."

"And?"

I crossed my arms. "And I've played Grand Theft Auto."

A slow smile crept across his face. "How in the world does that make you qualified to drive?"

I tapped my cheek. "Uh, let's see. I can outrun the cops, shoot a few bastards, and pick up a hooker, all at the same time. I'd say, I'm a woman of many skills."

He laughed, shook his head, and started to leave. "Now, that is talent."

I pushed his shoulder. "Now, get out of my seat before I pull your ass out and leave you on the side of the road."

"Not happening. Keep practicing with your video games, and we'll get you your permit."

I slumped back against my seat. "My permit? Seriously? What am I, twelve?"

"Yes, seriously, and it's fifteen when you get that."

I opened my clutch and pulled out a bill. "I'll give you ten dollars." I waved the money back and forth beside him.

He slowed down to stare at me "Really? You're trying to bribe me?"

"I sure am."

"Ten? You'd better up the ante."

"Fine." I pulled out another bill. "Eleven?"

His eyes widened. "Now, we're talking the big bucks. Give me twelve, and hell, you can have the whole car."

I busted out in laughter and pulled out another bill.

"And you just won a new car." He swiped the bills from my hand and shoved them into his pocket.

"You're so lying," I grumbled, holding out my hand. "Now, give me my money back."

"Not so fast there, babe."

I looked away as he turned onto an old, snow-covered road.

"I can't believe I'm doing this," he muttered, stopping the car.

I jumped out of the car before he had the chance to change his mind.

He held his hands into a steeple as soon as he got in next to me and stared up at the ceiling. "Lord," he said, his voice low, "please forgive me for my sins."

"What are you doing?" I asked, gripping the steering wheel.

"Praying for my life because I'm not so sure I'll be making it out of this alive."

"Very funny." I stretched the seat belt across my body. "Now, buckle up."

He did as he had been told and then turned around to peer at the backseat. "I knew I should've kept a helmet in here."

I shook my head at his comment and shifted the car into the D symbol. *That's drive, right?* Immediately after the light hit the D, I slammed my foot on the pedal, and we went flying forward.

"I am definitely going to die," he said when I used my other foot to press on the brakes.

My chest smacked into the steering wheel as we both swung forward.

He grabbed the door handle. "Maybe we should do this

another time—when it's not snowing and you know the basics of driving."

"I'm just testing you," I lied. I had no clue what I was doing.

His hands smacked into the dashboard when I braked again. "Right. I'm positive you've never even been behind a steering wheel, but we'll figure this out."

I brightened up. "Really?"

He nodded. "I'll talk you through it. Just lay easy on the pedals, and we might make it through this with a few limbs left." He shook his head. "And you've got me turning more reckless with each passing minute."

"Life's supposed to be reckless, Weston. It's not like it'll last forever anyway. We might as well make the best of it."

"True, but that doesn't mean I don't want it to last as long as possible." He grabbed the handle on the ceiling. "Now, ten and two."

"Ten and two? What the hell does that mean?"

His head fell back. "Ten and two are where you need to keep your hands on the wheel."

"Oh, right. I knew that."

I adjusted my hands until they were perfectly at *ten and two* and carefully pressed down on the accelerator. We shot forward.

"Good. Now, keep your hands on the wheel and drive at a very slow speed. Stop at fifteen miles per hour."

"This doesn't seem as fun as Grand Theft," I muttered, my foot tingling to press down and gain some speed.

He chuckled. "Gradually—and I mean, gradually—increase your speed. Just give the gas a little more pressure."

I gave it more gas. More gas than I probably should have. I shrieked as we went barreling down the street. My hands flew off the steering wheel when we started to slide.

Shit. Shit. Shit.

Maybe there was a reason I'd never driven before. I needed to stick to video games.

Weston stretched over me to grab the steering wheel and stopped us from landing in a ditch. We skidded to a stop as I threw my foot down onto the brakes.

"I think that's enough for today," he said, putting the car in park and blowing out a breath.

"So, how did I do?" I asked, smirking as we sat idle.

He tried to hide his smile but failed when he busted out in laughter. "I'd say, you failed. Rule number one: never let go of the steering wheel."

twenty-one

ELISE

Weston helped me out of the passenger seat and led me up a snowy footpath toward an aging brownstone building. I tucked myself into his side to block the bitter cold from smacking me in my face.

"What is this place?" I questioned, running my hands up and down my arms when we walked in.

The exterior was misleading to what was inside. It was spotless and in the process of being renovated. Dark mahogany wood covered the floor and led through the entry and down the hallway. Fresh taupe-colored paint coated the walls, and rows of mailboxes labeled with apartment numbers lined one.

"You'll see," he said, snatching my hand back up.

Each step creaked while he guided me up the stairs to apartment 2B.

"I thought we'd find a new and more creative way for you to express yourself today." He dug out a set of keys from his pocket and stuck one into the rusty lock, jiggling it a few times before it clicked open.

"A new what?" I already hated any form of expressing myself, so I doubted charting into new territory was going to make it any better.

"Patience is a virtue," he said.

I rolled my eyes. "I'm pretty sure I don't have any virtues."

That granted me a smile while he shook his head.

"Wow," I breathed out in awe when we walked inside.

We were standing in a small studio. The floor matched the one downstairs. It was sparsely furnished with only a single couch. Art took up most of the space.

Canvas after canvas, in multiple sizes, hung along the walls, were situated along the furniture, or carefully planted on the floor. I'd attended plenty of art shows with my father, but I didn't recognize the work. I realized they were familiar to the paintings at Weston's place.

"This is my friend's art studio," he told me, fussing with the thermostat until the furnace kicked on.

We both slipped out of our coats as soon as the place warmed up and draped them over the couch.

"They're breathtaking," I said, moving around the room, pausing to admire each piece.

The artist liked color. The pieces glowed with every hue in the spectrum, splashing together as one. I had to remind myself to breathe when I felt Weston's presence behind me.

"The artist is so talented," I whispered.

Breathe, Elise. Don't forget to breathe. I shivered when his cold breath hit my shoulder while he shadowed my steps.

I stopped abruptly at one piece in particular. For some reason, it completely drew me in. I inched closer, and my eyes squinted and scanned every inch of it. My hand went to my chest, and I gasped.

"She looks like me," I muttered, tilting my head to the side.

It was the largest painting in the room. A woman's face was

sketched wildly and filled with various shapes and colors to complete it.

"This one is my favorite," he said into my ear, his chest bumping into my back. "And you're right; she does remind me of you."

It was like I'd been the artist's muse. The woman in the painting had long black hair draped over the right side of her face. You could barely make out the dark features that were behind her. The right side—dark and depressing—contrasted with the right—filled with bright colors. Her blood-red lips started at a frown on the right and then morphed into a smile on the left.

She was contemplating whether to come out of her hiding. She was halfway there, unfolding that piece of her but hesitant on unraveling it all.

"She's stuck in two places," I told him.

"She is," he said.

I quivered when his hands skimmed down my sides and cradled my hips.

"She's thriving to be happy but scared at the same time. Is that what you see too?"

I nodded, my belly constricting. I was trying to focus on the picture, but the touch of his hands on me kept interrupting my line of thinking. "The right is her darkness. The left is her light."

"She's dark but innocent," he whispered, his voice thick and husky. The grip of his hands on my waist clamped tighter, causing goose bumps on my arms. "She's broken, but she's tough. She's a paradox, but she's an open book."

"She's one giant contradiction."

"No, she's a beautiful creature, trying to find her place in the world."

I shuddered when his lips nudged at my ear.

"Are you ready?"

139

His hands stayed put while I waited for him to elaborate on what I needed to be ready for, but he didn't care to fill me in.

"Ready for what?" I asked, the words squeaking out.

The hairs on my neck stood, and I suddenly felt chilly. The way his fingers lightly tapped on my hips and the feel of his tongue at my ear were making me delirious.

What is he asking me? His question had seemed so simple, but the meaning more complex. *Is he asking if I'm ready to partic-ipate in expressing myself? Or is he asking for permission to touch me more?*

I let out a rush of air when he released me and took a step back. I yelped when he turned me to face him. His fiery eyes latched on to my gaze intensely. This would be more than just our typical therapy session. I had a feeling we were going to be digging much deeper.

"I asked if you were ready," he repeated, testing me.

"I am," I lied.

"Then, let's go." His thumb jerked out, signaling toward the spiral steel staircase in the corner of the room.

My body briefly brushed against his chest as I walked around him. My heart raced with every step as I led the way until I finally landed in a loft. A long table covered with buckets of paint and paintbrushes was pushed up against a wall.

"This is where he does his magic," he said, walking around me and into the loft "He sees it as his therapy."

"And today, it's going to be mine?"

"It helps him. I have a feeling it'll do the same for you." He walked over to the table, popped a can of paint open, and grabbed a few wilted brushes from the aluminum canisters.

"And why do you think that?" I grabbed a paintbrush, feeling the dried-up paint linger against the tips of the fibers as I massaged the rough bristles. "And just so you know, I'm an atrocious artist. They wouldn't even hang up my pictures for the first-grade art show."

"It doesn't have to be beautiful to anyone but you. Art is a form of interpretation. You communicate your feelings through it. You surrender all your frustrations, your fears, your anger. You put it all out there until you feel cleansed."

"I'm telling you whatever I make will be far from beautiful," I grumbled.

"What it looks like doesn't matter. Take your anger out on it. Just like your life, it doesn't have to be beautiful. You only need to be happy with the strokes you make." He pulled a paint-splattered sheet from underneath the table and spread it across the floor. "Every stroke you make is different because every path you've walked is distinct. When my friend lost someone close to him, he didn't want to go to therapy, but he didn't want it to fester either, so he decided to use art as his release. It worked for him, so I thought you could try it. Talk about it with yourself if you don't want to talk about it with anyone else."

"I wish you had given me this option a long time ago," I said, my voice muffled.

He straightened the sheet on the floor, grabbed the easel nestled in the corner, and placed it on the sheet. Next, he placed a blank canvas onto the easel.

His deep-set, unrelenting eyes met mine when he turned around to give me directions. "Show me everything you have. Reveal your feelings from the inside out. Give me what eats at you and is seeping through your heart and veins, and I promise I will do everything I can to improve it."

My words caught in the back of my throat, struggling at the base, refusing to make their way up. I wanted to flee, but my legs were frozen in place. In the back of my mind, I knew I was lying to myself. I wanted to stay there and let Weston fix me.

Like the painting, I was stuck between two worlds, and it was time to decide whether to keep hiding or set myself free.

The sound of another paint can opening echoed through the mute air. My eyes set on him dipping a brush into the can. He dragged the brush across the canvas, creating a black streak.

His gaze leveled on me. "Show me the darkness inside you. Show me the light shining." He added a yellow streak over the black. Another can was popped open, and a red line joined the mix. "Show me the entirety of you."

I took a calming breath before moving his way and stopped in front of him, fear flooding through me. "And what about you?" I snagged the brush from him. "Why don't you do the same for me? Bare yourself, Weston. Let me see *your* darkness and what terrifies you."

He shook his head, glancing away from me as his small Adam's apple bobbed up and down. I stumbled backward, and his shoulder bumped into mine while he tried to maneuver around me. I snatched his arm and gripped his wrist forcefully to stop him.

"Your stories for mine," I said, holding up the brush.

I gasped when he jerked forward and pulled me into him. Our chests aligned, our mouths barely inches apart. I could feel the heat of our bodies colliding into one another's.

"What terrifies you?" I asked.

"You," he said, rasping it out.

My heart slammed against my rib cage. *What the hell is that supposed to mean?*

"You," he repeated, as if that one word was supposed to explain everything.

"What?" I choked out.

"You are what terrifies me."

His confession seemed to shock the both of us.

"I'm what terrifies you?" I asked.

And it dawned on me. I was wrecking him. He wanted me. The only man I'd ever dreamed about wanting me did, but we couldn't do anything about it. His want for me tortured him. I was his weakness. I was the sinner lying next to him at night, tempting him with forbidden desire. And that made me feel terrible.

I took a step back, finding the strength in my body to move, but it was his turn to stop me. He didn't say anything. He only stood there, keeping his hold on me, while we both internally fought with ourselves. We were starving, ravenous, but too terrified to take that first bite, scared it would turn us into gluttons for each other and we'd never stop.

"Let me finish," he demanded.

"You don't have to finish," I said, my eyes falling to the floor. "I'm sorry."

He caught my chin between his thumb and forefinger and stroked it. "Don't be sorry, and please don't leave."

His caress relaxed me. He lifted my chin higher before grabbing me around the waist and walking me backward. We stopped next to the paint cans, and he dipped a finger into a bucket, playing with the liquid on his fingers.

"You're my work," he said, tracing my bottom lip with color while I stared up at him, transfixed. "You're the one person I'm not supposed to want. The person I'm not supposed to crave. It's forbidden for me to want you like I do. I have to resist taking you right here, no matter how badly I want to, because it's wrong. I shouldn't want you like this, but I can't help it."

His hand returned to the paint pot as I struggled to breathe. He covered his palm with red paint and placed it across my cheek.

"I lose all my sanity, rationality, my principles when I'm with you. I forget to think. I'm reckless. Every rule in my head is broken and replaced with my feelings for you."

I held on to him, feeling the cold liquid drip down my cheek and onto the sheet, while his words sank in. "Out of everything in this crazy world," I said, tasting the paint on my lips, "I'm what scares you? I'm your forbidden fruit?"

He nodded, his hand stroking my cheek and then descending my neck. "You are, and I'd eat the entire apple as long as it tasted like you."

twenty-two

ELISE

He stared at me, battling with himself and deciding if I was worth the risk.

I pushed away any lingering doubts. I'd made my mind up. I undisputedly wanted him and didn't care if he was forbidden. I stood up on my tiptoes to graze my lips against his.

"This isn't a good idea," he muttered.

I could feel the hard air of his breathing pushing against my lips. "To hell with good ideas," I whispered.

He trembled when I slid a hand to the back of his neck to hold him in place. I moved my tongue along his lips, testing to see how he'd react. My body warmed when his tongue slid into my mouth. The taste of cinnamon and paint blended on my tongue.

A deep growl broke from his chest when I bit into his plump bottom lip, capturing it with my teeth. He deepened our kiss, his lips claiming mine as he'd always owned them. My veins pulsed, shooting all my blood to the center of my thighs. His fingers curled around my waist and put deep pressure on my sensitive skin while he walked me backward.

I grew wobbly, almost falling on my ass, and he settled me on top of the sheet. I struggled to pull myself onto my elbows, wanting to watch his every move, but he pulled away from me. He put the paint cans and brushes in his arms and dropped them beside me.

"Let's not forget the task at hand," he said in amusement, kneeling at my side. "I said you'd be expressing yourself today. That's what we're going to do."

My eyes turned wild, unable to focus on anything but him, and his hand dipped underneath my T-shirt. I shivered at the feel of his palm splaying across my stomach, and he started to move it in circles. My skin quivered as I silently begged for more. I was only interested in expressing myself with him inside me.

"I think I like this form of expression," I said, gasping when his strong hand palmed my breast. "But I think we need to dig a little deeper, get a little more personal."

He bent forward to push my hair back and ran a finger along my cheek. I felt the weight of his body when he climbed over me, his eyes burning with dominance, and he straddled my thighs. The hard bulge between his legs nudged against where I needed it.

Then, it hit me.

Weston's gaze snapped to me when I frantically grabbed his hand. "Do you want me to stop?" he asked, scooting away from me. "I'll stop. I'm sorry."

"No," I said, not wanting him to stop. I only needed to make one *minor* adjustment. "I need to be on top. I have to be on top. I don't do bottom."

Never had I willingly allowed sex missionary, doggy style, or any other way. Call me boring, but the only way I took dick was how I wanted it—riding it. No Kama Sutra, no reverse cowgirl, just plain old dick-riding was my specialty, and that wasn't open for discussion. When I agreed to have sex, it was my choice to say how I wanted it.

He pulled away, and paint spread through his curls when he ran his hands through them. "This isn't going to happen. I won't touch you anymore if you don't trust me."

I warred with myself, trying to muster up my best argument, but I couldn't focus. I ached for his hands to be back on me, his skin on mine, and decided I needed that more than I needed to be in control.

I'd lose him if I didn't tell him what he wanted to hear. He'd stop if I didn't validate how I felt for him. He wouldn't go there with me until he knew I trusted him and didn't see him as a product to make myself feel better. He wouldn't let me use him like I had other guys.

I placed my finger into the paint can. "I trust you. I completely trust you," I lied, running a streak of red paint down his arm.

"Thank God," he growled, kissing me.

The only thing he wanted from me was the hardest for me to give.

Trust.

He hastily dragged my shirt over my head, my declaration empowering and exciting him more, and tossed it to the side. Next was my bra. Butterflies swarmed through my stomach as I watched his hungry eyes fasten on my bare breasts. He scooted in closer between my thighs and used his elbow to spread open my legs.

My back arched at the feeling of the cold liquid floating along my stomach and circling around my breast. The brush tickled like sparks crackling across my skin. The only sounds in the room were the unsnapping of my jeans and our heavy breathing. I hiked my ass up, assisting him in pulling off my jeans, and then kicked them off my heels.

"You're breathtaking," he whispered, licking his lips and then going silent.

He used his hands to express himself. His five fingers, like weapons, generated everything he wanted to say. I waited underneath him while he created his masterpiece. My skin was his canvas, and he awakened all my senses simultaneously.

The bristles of the brush combined with the soft *touch* of his fingers set me ablaze. I *tasted* the lacquer on my tongue. I *watched* him concentrate on me, like he was being paid millions for his creation. The *scent* of chemicals dragged through the air, engulfing my nostrils. The *sound* of our low, steady breathing echoed around the room.

He worked meticulously, taking his time to focus on my most sensitive spots. "Can I kiss you here?" he asked, tossing the brush to the side, his cold hands roaming my inner thighs.

"Yes, please," I pleaded. "You can kiss me anywhere you'd like, but definitely there, yes."

He grinned before lowering his head. I lifted myself, watching him ease his hand underneath my panties and slide a finger through my warmth. I wanted him to lick me. I wanted his tongue between my legs, lapping me up, and then I wanted him inside me.

"Whoa, eager one," he chuckled when I tilted my hips up to meet his touch. "Patience." He took off his glasses and rested them at the top of his head.

"To hell with patience," I muttered, pulling my panties down my legs hastily.

I let out a moan when he spread me wider. I bucked my hips forward, liquid pouring between my legs when he met my folds. His breath caught in his throat, his face scrunching when he felt how soaked I was for him.

"I thought you were going to have your mouth there," I said, my voice shaky.

"Lie back," he whispered, a hand going to my chest to push me down. "I'm going to take care of you."

His fingers went to work between my legs, touching me everywhere but where I needed it most. The hand resting on my chest wrapped around my needy breast, and my back arched when he flicked a nipple.

"What the hell are you doing to me?" I asked.

"I'm going to make you feel good," he told me confidently. "I'm going to make you feel more and come harder than any of those men you've used."

I thrummed with pleasure when he drove a finger inside me, using the tip to tease me. Just a single finger in and out, hitting every nerve ending in his path. My body was completely receptive to his every touch. He added another tentative finger, pumping inside me, and my head fell back.

That feels amazing.

I yelped, my mouth flying open, when his tongue joined his fingers. He used them in intervals, replacing one with the other repeatedly.

"Keep doing that," I gasped, moving my hips to meet him.

I sighed when he removed his fingers, one by one, until his tongue was the only thing between my legs.

"I love the way you taste," he said, his voice vibrating against my pussy while he moved a finger to my clit.

I made noises in the back of my throat as he sucked and licked me. His hand pulled away from my breast, causing me to whimper, but I grinned when he used it to lift my hips closer to meet his mouth. I tried to hold back, wanting to turn my body down so this could last longer, but it was all too much. His tongue was devouring me, his finger toyed with my clit, and the view of his head shoved between my legs was exhilarating. I snapped up when a thousand waves moved through me and hit me in places I'd never known possible.

"Holy fucking shit!" I screamed, my head spinning when I let out my release. I gripped his hair, needing something to hold on to while my body spiraled out of control.

His lips brushed against each thigh before he lifted to stare at me. He grinned triumphantly, licking his lips, and slid his finger, covered with my juices, between them.

"You, my dear, taste fantastic," he said. "Even better than I imagined."

"You've imagined eating me out?" I asked, coming down from my high.

"More times than you think."

"Oh, really? Do go on."

"That will have to wait until I'm inside you, taking you slowly and whispering every fantasy I've ever had of you before I act them out."

I gulped. "How about we do that now?"

He shook his head. "Not yet. We're not ready."

He picked me up, carried me down the stairs, and into the bathroom. He set me down on the closed toilet seat and turned on the shower. My jaw dropped when he stripped off his clothes. My eyes stayed glued on him, and I waited in anticipation for him to turn around and show me every inch of him. Unfortunately, he didn't give me time to stare. Instead, he swept me up, and I frowned when he planted me in the shower.

He stood behind me, and the water rushed down on us as he scrubbed away the paint on my skin. It felt so intimate.

"So, how did I do in therapy today?" I asked. "Did I express myself well?"

He chuckled, massaging masculine-scented shampoo into my hair. "You did amazing. You are phenomenal."

I pulled away and attempted to turn around and face him,

but he wouldn't let me. I wanted to see, kiss, and feel him, but he held me back. I pushed my ass into him, deciding to play dirty, and moaned when I felt his hard cock rub against it.

"Nuh-uh, love," he whispered in my ear, taking a step back and disrupting my seduction plan. "Today is about you, not me."

"I showed you mine; it's only fair I see yours," I whined.

He let out a breath, rinsed my hair out, and then turned me around. My stomach flipped, my nipples going erect, as I took him in. His eyes glistened as I peered at him in surprise. My attention darted south before he got the chance to decide it was time for me to turn around.

His firm, muscular chest heaved in and out. He was fit—like really fit—with muscles finely sculpted into his stomach. I tilted my head to the side and admired my view.

I lowered my gaze to his firm cock. It was thick and perfect. I could feel myself growing wet, seeing it twitch under the running water. "You're huge. You should be bragging about that."

He swiped wet hair from my face. "It might be a little weird bragging about the size of my cock."

"Men do it all the time."

"Not me. I don't want to be known for my cock. I want to be known for something more than my body."

"So do I," I whispered.

He leaned down to kiss my forehead. "You are."

twenty-three

ELISE

"How many girls have you had sex with?" I asked, throwing up my arms for Weston to pull my shirt over my head after drying me off.

He kissed me on the forehead before reaching for his jeans. "I think that's irrelevant."

"Not really." I pulled back my wet hair and wrapped it up around my hand. "You know my sexual history. I think it's only fair I know yours."

He buckled his jeans and then looked away from me. "Five."

I dropped my hair in shock. "Five? That's it? You've only had sex with *five* women, and you're how old?"

"Twenty-eight." His answer was muffled as he dragged his shirt over his head.

"Wow," I said loudly, drawing the word out. "I feel like a total whore."

His eyebrows crushed together. "Don't say that." He grabbed my hand, helped me to my feet, and then smoothed my hair.

"I'm eight years younger than you, and I've had more than four times as many sexual partners. If that's not slutty, I don't know what is. No wonder everyone thinks I'm a whore."

I had known my number was high, but not *that* out of the ordinary. Holly followed me close behind, and most of the men I knew were just as bad, if not worse. I wasn't used to being around a man who didn't whip his cock out to every willing woman around.

"You're not a slut. Don't compare yourself to me. I've been in long-term relationships," he said to make me feel better. "I've had plenty of sex, but it was with girlfriends."

Not with random people, like I have.

"All of them? You've never cheated?" I asked.

He flinched, insulted. "Never," he said harshly. "That's not me. I don't sleep around or have one-night stands. If I'm sleeping with someone, I'm committed to her. Remember that."

twenty-four

ELISE

"Cancel your appointments, Doctor. I'm the only one you're making feel better today," I sang, sluggishly lifting myself to straddle Weston's hips.

It was my fifth morning in his bed.

It was strange. It was weird.

It was pleasantly strange and weird.

When I was with Weston, my life seemed normal. I'd never experienced normal. I wasn't sure what we were to each other or where we were headed, but I was going along for the ride until he decided to throw me out. I was holding on to whatever he was willing to give if it meant I could stay in his bed and his life.

It was terrifying to admit, but I was falling in love with him. There was no denying it. His presence made me feel protected and safe. I didn't want him to go anywhere, but I knew, ultimately, he'd end up leaving me. Whenever I thought my life was beginning to look up, I missed a step and came barreling back down. So, I decided I would take every piece of him I could get in our time together before he discovered all the darkness inside me.

He yawned loudly and squinted a few times to focus on me since he wasn't wearing his glasses. I grinned at him while my stomach flip-flopped. His curls were a mess, matted down against the pillow. I ran my palms along his smooth, bare chest, excitement hitting me when I noticed the rising goose bumps. I loved having that effect on him. I loved that he wanted me as bad as I wanted him.

"I wish I could, love," he groaned. "But I have appointments with new patients."

"Reschedule them," I suggested, nudging my hips against him, feeling the fullness of his morning erection through my panties. I wanted him to know what he'd be getting if he stayed and what he'd be missing out on if he left.

He opened his eyes, fully alert, and tipped his hips forward. I dropped my head back, remembering the things he'd done to me at the art studio.

I'd practically begged him to take me last night, but he wouldn't budge. He had gotten me off with his fingers again and then said it was time for bed. Apparently, we needed to take baby steps, but that wasn't what I wanted. I wanted us to go right in and hit a homerun.

I squealed and tightened my legs around his waist when he planted a hand on my side. He bunched up my T-shirt—well, his T-shirt—to get a firm grip on me and rolled his hips. My pussy tingled at our friction.

"Trust me, I want you, but you'll have to wait, beautiful," he said, his eyes devilish. He was teasing me.

"I love it when you call me beautiful," I whispered.

"You are beautiful." He moved his hand to my face, brought it to his, and nuzzled my nose before brushing his lips against the tip. "You're beautiful here." He kissed me again. "And here."

His hand flew underneath my shirt, squeezing my bare breast before kneading it with his knuckle, and I shimmied. "And I think you're beautiful here." His hand moved to my thumping heart.

"Is there anywhere else you think I'm beautiful?" I asked, raising a brow.

A slow, mischievous grin grew on his face. I shivered, feeling his morning stubble itch at my neck as he kissed his way up my skin. His hand loosened at my hip to skim underneath the blanket covering our bottom halves.

A moan escaped me when he gripped my ass and used it to push me down harder against his throbbing cock. There was no way I was letting him leave. I tilted my hips back, feeling every inch of him slide against my pussy, letting him know I was game for anything.

He slapped my ass, inching my legs farther apart. I stared at him in awe, anxiousness humming through me when his fingers dipped under the lace of my panties. His touch was hot as he caught my clit between his fingers, playing with my sensitive nub.

He nudged my hips up to give him more reach. "You're soaked, baby," he said, playing with my aching pussy.

I took off my shirt and tossed it on the floor. The room was suddenly burning up.

I grunted when I was pulled off his lap and thrown onto my back, and he hovered above me.

"I'd love to spend all morning playing with this sexy body, but we don't have time for that right now."

His lips slipped over mine, and he sucked on my tongue before sliding down my body. In one swift motion, my panties were gone, and his mouth was between my legs. He dived straight in, not taking his time as he spread me open and drove his tongue into me. And I was completely fine with that. I would've been perfectly content, lying in his bed with his tongue inside me for the rest of my life.

"So wet," he muttered between licks. "So wet and so good."

"Show me one of your fantasies."

My breaths were long, releasing out in urgency and pleasure. I watched him lick me and rewarded him with a moan after each tongue stroke. Sweat dripped down his forehead, landing on my clit, and it excited me more. I lost my concentration on him, my brain going hazy when he plunged a finger inside me.

He was licking me. He was fingering me. He was toying with my clit. All at the same time. A triple threat. I was done for. I was positive this man also had a Ph.D. in eating pussy.

"Okay, okay," I said, my hand shooting to his hair, pulling it tight. "Weston, you're killing me! God, so good."

I threw my head back, keeping my hold on his hair, and my core throbbed as my body let go. I fell hard until I came to a complete crash.

He kissed his way back up my stomach. "I'm sorry. What were you saying?" he asked with a smirk. "I was busy at the moment."

I smacked his shoulder while slowly regaining control of my body. "You were torturing me."

He grinned. "I wasn't going to stop until you were a sweaty, sticky, shaking mess." He observed me up and down. "Which it looks like you are."

"How come you get to have all of the fun?" I asked, pouting my lips and pulling at his shorts.

His forehead collapsed against my belly as he stopped my hand. "I have to go to work."

"Screw me, then go to work," I begged.

"I'm not going to have sex with you and then leave right after."

"Yes, you are," I said, tugging at his shorts and cursing when he stopped me *again*. I leaned forward and sank my teeth into his arm.

"Ouch," he said, expecting the indent in the shape of my teeth in his arm. "What the hell?"

"Quit stopping me, or I'll bite you again. *Harder.*"

He shook his head. "No. I'm not like those other guys. I'm not going to treat you like that. I'm not going to have sex with you and then leave."

So, it was definitely going to happen. Sooner or later, we were going to have sex. The big question was when, and if I had any say in it, it was right now.

"Shut up. You know you'll never be one of those guys," I said, kissing the bite mark on his arm.

When I went for his shorts this time, he didn't stop me.

"You know," I said with a smug smile. "They say that morning sex was proven to be more effective than a cup of coffee."

I grabbed his bulging cock in my hand and wrapped my fingers around it before sliding them up and down his length. I knew I'd won when his head fell back in pleasure.

"Oh, really?" he asked, panting while pumping up his hips to meet my touch. His balls smacked into my belly. "I promise, as soon as I get back, we can test that theory as much as you want."

His hand swept between us so he could drum a finger against my clit.

Hell to the no. There was no way I was letting him leave. "It will be too late."

"Jesus ..." His voice was strangled as he began to play with me. "You're already soaked again."

He was right. I could feel my juices smearing between my thighs.

"Please ..." I begged.

"Please what?" he asked, sliding his cock out of my hold.

"Fuck me. I don't care if it's only five seconds—"

"Yeah, that's not going to happen—*ever*," he interrupted.

"I need you inside me." I moved my hips to meet his hand, slightly hitting his balls.

He pulled back, eyeing me. "Are you sure?"

"I've never been so sure of anything in my life."

He moved over my body to pull a condom from the nightstand drawer. I held my breath, positive I was going to pass out and not get the chance to enjoy him inside me. He rolled the condom on his stiff cock before nudging it back and forth along my opening, saturating the condom with my juices as he teased me.

He held my gaze as he steadily entered me. I constricted against him, taking a moment to adjust to his size.

"You're so big," I gasped.

"Do you like it?" he asked, thrusting in and out of me before kissing me deep and rough.

I tasted myself on his tongue, and it felt so erotic. I whimpered at the loss of his mouth when he bent down to suck on a nipple. "You know I do."

My head bowed back, and I got lost in the feeling of him petting me from the inside. I enjoyed every inch of him sliding in and out of me, him sucking on my nipple and how he thrived on how good it felt to be inside me.

"This was one of my fantasies," he said. "You in my bed."

"Mine too," I said, my throat dry. "I've imagined you doing so many things to me here."

He groaned, his pace quickening, and I knew he was close. *Thank God* because I was about there. I rammed my hips up to meet his thrusts, scratching my nails down his back, and he reached down to hitch my leg up around his hip.

His fingers dug into my skin, sinking in deeper with each powerful plunge. He stared at my bouncing breasts as my brain flooded with pure bliss.

"I want this to last forever," I said, knowing I was close.

"Trust me, it will be happening again," he muttered.

His words were my undoing.

The fact that he'd said he'd be inside me again set me off. My entire body went limp, shaking while he continued to fuck me. When he found his release, he shoved his face into my neck and shuddered against my skin.

"You're right. That was much better than coffee," he said, kissing me on the lips.

I rotated my hips, still feeling him inside me. "I told you."

He slightly frowned. "I'm sorry. I wanted our first time to be more special than that."

"That's exactly how I wanted it."

I hadn't wanted him to make a big ordeal about it. I'd wanted it to be spur of the moment, dirty, and unplanned. I'd wanted him to leave his comfort zone.

And that was exactly what he'd done.

twenty-five

WESTON

I slammed my office door shut as soon as my last patient left. Adrenaline pumped through me like a drug as I raced home. I couldn't wait to get back to Elise. I'd only been gone for eight hours, but those eight hours had been excruciating. All day, I'd sat in my chair, licking my lips so I could keep tasting her, and tried my hardest to listen to my patients.

I stopped at a red light and thrummed my fingers to the beat of the music when it dawned on me. I was in love with her. Elise was everything to me. She was my first thought when I woke up and my last before I went to bed. She'd taken over me.

Even though I'd only known her for a short time, I knew it wasn't lust. It was love. There was no denying it. I'd tried to fight it but kept getting slammed back whenever she looked at me.

I knew she was off-limits but no longer cared. I was done trying to convince myself I couldn't have her. I'd stopped trying to change my mind. No more battling with myself. I'd taken all my rules and kicked them out the door.

When I walked into my apartment, my briefcase made a *thud*, falling to the floor at the same time my jaw dropped open.

Elise was sitting on the edge of the couch, wearing one of my T-shirts. Her hair was pulled into a messy ponytail. Her legs were open wide, giving me the best view I'd ever seen—her bare pussy on display for me.

My cock twitched, instantly stirring to life, and I couldn't drag my eyes away from her. I felt like a kid who'd just watched porn for the first time.

"Did you have a good day at work?" she asked, grinning mischievously. She slanted her back and used her fingers to open herself up more—an invitation for me to explore every inch of her.

I loosened my tie. "I have a feeling it's about to get a hell of a lot better." Charging over and slamming inside her sounded like a good plan, but I stopped myself. I wanted to play first. "Show me how you touched yourself that night on the phone." I started unbuckling my pants.

Her eyes fired up at the challenge. "You go; I go."

I dropped my pants in seconds and wrapped my hand around my swollen cock. My gaze stayed focused on her as I pumped my dick once, and I released the cockiest grin I'd ever made when I noticed her shallow breathing growing heavy. "Your turn."

I was going to enjoy her reenactment. I was more of a visual type of guy.

Her tongue slid over her bottom lip, and my hand clenched around my cock when she reached down and feathered her fingers between her thighs.

"Was it just one finger I was allowed?" she asked before holding up a single finger at her entrance. She circled it around and then moved it to point my way.

"Just one," I croaked out.

She glided a finger around her opening before pushing it inside herself. Sweat built along my forehead as I stroked my cock faster, and I tore my shirt off with my free hand.

Multitasking at its finest.

She used one finger like I'd instructed, dipping it in and out of her core. I struggled to breathe when I noticed her juices dripping between her legs and onto the couch's armrest.

We locked eyes, the tempo of our hands in synchronization. I was on fire, surprised I could even stand when she added another finger. Her hand was slick and steady. *In and out.* I pumped my cock. *Up and down.*

I lost all my power when she twisted a nipple with her free hand. I dropped my hand and moved forward. Her skin burned against my touch when I reached her. I slipped my fingers inside her wet pussy, feeling them rub against her fingertips as we pleased her together. Her back arched, her ass almost falling off the edge of the couch, and I pulled her fingers out.

She groaned when I grabbed her hips to lower us onto the couch. I propped a foot onto the floor, settling my knee to her side to balance myself, and that gave me the perfect angle to play with her pussy.

I salivated, watching her squirm beneath me. Her breasts jiggled with every thrust of my finger and begged for attention. Her hand went to my neck, holding me tight, when my mouth wrapped around her hard pink nipple. My tongue swirled around the tiny peak, and I lightly flicked it. I allowed her to set the speed on how she wanted me to give it to her.

"You have the body of an angel," I said, tearing my mouth away.

She shivered as I dragged my hand down her body, between her breasts, and stroked her clit. Her hair was tangled up underneath her neck, tendrils falling from her ponytail and over her eyes.

"Just fuck me already," she hissed.

"And the mouth of a sailor," I said, chuckling.

"Trust me," she breathed out, lifting her chin, "this mouth is much more advanced than a sailor's." She gripped my neck to slam our lips back together. "Let me show you."

Her hand splayed out on my stomach, and I grunted when she pushed me back. She fell forward on her knees. When she took me in her mouth, sucking me, my hips rocked forward, my mouth shooting open. I lost all my focus, not hearing a word she was muttering against my cock while she worked me in and out.

I pulled her ponytail loose, snatching a handful of her soft hair, and pumped my hips. I was so close, but I wasn't doing it without her.

She yelped when I pulled away from her, grabbed her hips to hoist her up, and quickly sank her on my cock. I kissed her and held her gaze as she started to ride me. I felt every inch of her as we rocked against each other.

I growled, grabbing her breasts and squeezing them, while she impaled herself with me over and over again. Her pussy took my cock, her ass smacked against my thighs, and our bodies worked together to pleasure each other.

Her head fell back, her skin shivering as we lost all our inhibitions. I wanted to move us from the couch. I wanted to pick her up and plant her in my bed, but I gave her what she wanted. I was handing over my body and letting her do it her way. And she loved it.

She shuddered around me, her moans growing louder as she rode me. I grunted with each thrust, staring down and watching her slide up and down my dick.

"I'm close," she whispered, her dark eyes staring down at me with fire as she picked up the pace.

I snatched her hips, roughly pushing her down on me, and exploded inside her as we both let out our release.

twenty-six

ELISE

All my energy had been drained from my body. My chest smacked into Weston's when I slumped and gave him all my weight.

His lips smacked into my forehead. "I'll be right back," he said, carefully lifting me from his lap.

He gently settled me onto the couch and then headed into the bedroom. My legs shook as I focused on leveling my breathing.

"Let's go," he said, coming back into the living room, still naked, his limp cock bouncing with every step.

I let out a whimper when he picked me up from the couch, pulled me into his arms, and carried me to the bathroom. The only light was from the flickering of scented candles, and the bath was full with water and bubbles.

"Is this okay?" he asked.

I gave him a small smile. "This is perfect." I ran my hands up his chest and raised to kiss him. "This is perfect."

He carefully lifted me into the bathtub. Since my legs were

somewhat wobbly and sore, the warm water felt good on my body. My eyes stayed on him as he climbed in and settled down, facing me.

"Question," I said.

He tilted his head to the side and waited for me to continue.

"How did you learn to use your tongue like that?"

He chuckled, shaking his head. "I hope you're not truly expecting me to answer that."

"Oh, I truly am."

He stretched his arms out to rest them on my legs. "It's not necessary, learning how to do it. It's being attentive. I want to make sure you enjoy yourself as much as I'm enjoying you. It's harder for women to get off *and* unfair to think of only yourself in bed, so I make it a goal to be the last one to come."

I bit the edge of my lip. "So, the whole *nice guys finish last* saying is true?"

"Damn straight." He wrapped his hands around my waist to bring me closer.

I wiggled my ass against the bottom of the tub in a lame attempt to pull away. "Nope, I want an answer. You're trying that psychological bullshit to take my mind away from the question at hand. I know you've had plenty of practice. It's not basic instinct to be able to use your tongue like that. So, spill."

Other guys had attempted to eat me out, and I hated it. Their droopy, soggy lips had felt awkward on me for the few seconds they actually tried.

He kissed me, then dragged a handful of bubbles across my cheek. "My first serious girlfriend wanted to wait until she was a senior before we had sex, but she let me do other things to her."

"Ahhh ..." I grinned a sly smile. "So, you ate her out as much as you could?"

He nodded, rolling his eyes. "Pretty much, yes."

I ran my hands up his arms. "Well, if you ever talk to her again, tell her I said thank you."

He threw his head back, laughing. "If I talk to her again, I don't think it would be appropriate for me to talk to her about how I used to eat her pussy. She's married to a friend."

"Oh. Then, I guess that's not a good idea."

"My turn. Did you sleep with your other therapists?"

I shrank. I liked to ask him personal questions, but I hated when he did the same. "Just one, but it wasn't technically sleeping with him. He fingered me twice, and that's it. He ended up feeling guilty about it and told on himself. I only told you that because I was pissed that they'd replaced Patterson with you."

He dragged his hand along his forehead. "Not sure if I like that."

I gave him a weak smile. *A subject change is needed.* "Have you lived here your entire life?"

He nodded.

"Had you heard about me before we met?"

His brows arched. He seemed to be curious about where I was going with this. "Vaguely. When I met you at Sun Gate, I had no idea. I went to college on the East Coast, and I didn't follow gossip. I'm also eight years older than you. Your name might've been mentioned, but I never paid attention." He paused. "Why do you care?"

"Huh?"

"Those people, the gossipers who don't know the truth, forget them. Quit caring." He dragged me back to him. "You know, you can always open up about your story. It's not too late."

I played with his wet hair. "As weird as it sounds, it would put me through more pain to do that. I want to let it go and move on."

"I understand. If you ever change your mind, I'm here for you. I'll always be here for you."

I suddenly felt nervous and fumbled for the right words before looking away from him. "You're the only one I've told everything to."

His face turned soft. "I know and thank you for trusting me. You have no idea how much that means to me."

"I'm letting you in," I whispered. "Please don't hurt me."

"That's something you never need to worry about."

twenty-seven

ELISE

"You answer that, you die," I threatened when I heard the doorbell ring. I circled my arms around Weston's back and nuzzled my face in the heat of his soft chest to stop him.

He chuckled and leaned down to kiss the top of my head. "Do you ignore people who ring your doorbell?"

I rested my chin on his chest and stroked my fingers over the ridge of his muscles. "I never had people ringing my doorbell. Visitors weren't a regular occurrence at my place apart from Holly. I always left to meet ..." I slammed my mouth shut when I realized what I had been about to say.

His eyes darkened. "Left to meet ..."

"Uh ... people?"

Men. The answer was men. I'd always left to meet *men.* They never came over. I wouldn't risk my father running them off if they weren't from the perfect pedigree. Even if they were, I never knew what mood he'd be in. So, I'd meet them, take what I wanted, and leave.

"To meet guys," he clarified.

Nervousness blossomed in my chest, and my answer was rushed out. "You know my history."

"Whoa, whoa," he said, stopping me from my impending freak-out. "You don't have to explain anything to me. You have a past. We both do. I'm not mad, nor do I look down on you for your choices. You didn't do anything wrong. You're you, and I wouldn't want you any other way, you got that? I love everything about you."

"You have a past? What? A holy saint one?"

He was going to need a baptism after he was done with me.

"Believe me, darling, I've regretted plenty stuff I've done. I'm no saint."

"Like what? What could you possibly regret?" *Or who?*

"Just things. Not important," he said sharply, clearly not in the mood to continue the discussion.

The doorbell rang again.

Weston groaned while I spewed a string of other curses. "Whoever it is, they aren't planning on going away."

"Whoever it is, don't get mad if I punch them in the face," I whined. "Or kill them."

His lips hit my hair before he climbed out of bed and gave me the best view *ever*. My mouth watered while I watched him collect his clothes in all his glory.

"Come back to bed, and I promise you won't regret it," I said, licking my lips and tapping the space next to me.

He glanced down at his cock and then at me. "Quit talking like that, or whoever is on the other side of that door will be graced with my hard-on." He chuckled as I groaned out in frustration. "I'll be back to give it to you."

I fell back against the bed. "Then, hurry up and get them the hell out of here."

He shook his head, still laughing, and got dressed. The

doorbell rang again, and I jumped at the ear-splitting sound of his phone ringing next to the bed.

"Somebody had better be dead," I muttered, picking up a pillow and tossing it on top of the phone.

"I'll be right back," he said, ignoring his phone and shutting the bedroom door behind him as he left.

I jumped out of bed and headed toward the bathroom. I grabbed my toothbrush, brushed my teeth, and was headed back to bed when I heard voices outside the door. Three of them, but I only focused on one. A heavy numbness infiltrated my stomach.

No. No. No.

"Go get her," the burning voice on the other side of the door demanded.

My father's voice.

I settled my trembling hands against the wall while trying to figure out my next move.

"Hell no," Weston spat, and I could tell he was trying to keep his voice low. "You're lucky I'm not kicking your ass or calling the cops after what you did to her. After *everything* you've done to her. You don't deserve to speak to her."

This isn't happening.

"Just do what he says," an unrecognizable voice added. "Whatever you have going on with his daughter, it's inappropriate, and you know it. The last thing you need is your reputation and our name to be contaminated because you couldn't keep your dick in your pants. There are plenty of women out there."

"Bring her out here!" my father yelled.

"No, I think she should stay in there," the unrecognized man argued. "Tell her to get her things and Weston will drop her off at home."

The floor creaked as footsteps came closer.

"Is this where she is?" my father asked. "Is this your bedroom? You son of a bitch!"

I sprinted away from the door and rifled through my bag. I hurriedly stepped into a pair of panties, got dressed, and stormed into the living room. I wasn't going to give him the chance to barge in on me and drag me out of the bedroom. I was going to confront him face-to-face, stand my ground, and let him know I wasn't going anywhere.

"You listen here," I screamed, erupting through the doorway.

All the air punched from my lungs in a painful rush when I caught sight of the three men arguing. I held my chest to control my breathing and shut my eyes, praying I was stuck in a nightmare.

There was Weston.

My father.

The other man, I hadn't seen him in years, but I'd never forget this face.

Never.

I stumbled back, shaking.

"No," I muttered repeatedly. The high I'd been riding this morning was completely shattered, and I was getting shredded with the pieces.

Weston rushed to my side and grabbed my arm to stabilize me before I fell to my knees. "Don't worry. I'll get your father out of here. Go back to the bedroom, and I'll be right there."

He didn't get it.

I wanted both of them out of there.

I pointed at the man standing in front of my father. "It's you."

Everyone gaped at me in shock and stayed silent while waiting for my next move.

"Why are you here?" I screamed.

The man's face paled and hardened at the same time. His jaw ticked as he directed his eyes downward.

"Look at me, you goddamn bastard!" I shouted, shocked I wasn't foaming at the mouth from all my built-up resentment toward him.

Everyone else in the room dissipated as I fixed my eyes on him.

He'd aged in the years since I'd seen him. His eyes were still cold and predatory and reminded me of the day he'd wandered into my bedroom. He was fatter. Thick wrinkles expanded along his forehead, and bags were under his eyes.

But even with the aging, there was no disputing who he was.

And he knew I knew.

"Huh?" Weston's voice broke through the silence. "What's going on?"

No one dared to make a move or sputter a word. Even my father was smart enough to keep his mouth shut while contemplating his next action. If I answered Weston's question, it could never be undone.

I shook my head in anger.

Why did my father bring him here?

Was this all part of his ploy to get me to come home?

My father was always one step ahead of me, and I was terrified of what he had up his sleeve today.

"Have the girl go home with her father, Weston," the man I hated said, his voice squeaking with each syllable. "I have a meeting to attend." He cleared his throat. "I'll call you later."

He didn't dare meet my eyes once. He couldn't. He had no backbone. A man who abused women was like a jellyfish. He had no spine and did nothing but sting his prey, inflicting them with pain, and then hurrying away like a pussy.

The man wasn't looking at me or my father. He was focused

on Weston.

My gaze flickered away from him to Weston. "How do you know him?"

A cold, malicious laugh bellowed from my father's throat as he eyed everyone with amusement. We were his entertainment for the day. He'd been waiting for the perfect moment. This was it. He'd destroy every block lifting me up and away from him, so I'd fall helplessly back into his lap.

"Oh, Mickey," he said mockingly. "I think we all need to stay right here." His attention went to Weston. "It seems my daughter has been aquatinted with every man in this room at some point in her life."

"Fuck you!" I spat.

"What is he talking about?" Weston asked, his head bobbing in every direction, like he was trying to figure out the puzzle. He finally stopped his gaze on me.

I struggled to find the right words. They were on the tip of my tongue but refusing to spew out.

My father's lips screwed into a crooked smile, and I knew Weston would get his answer whether I told him or not. My body began to overheat, and I lost Weston's hold as I stumbled back against the wall for support.

My father was going to get me home, no matter what. He looked at Mickey. "I think it's time for honest hour since it seems your son is screwing my daughter."

Wait. What?

No. No. No.

It was not possible that a guy as great as Weston could be the spawn of that monster. I couldn't keep track of the endless emotions hammering through my heart and speeding up to my brain. This was my breaking point. This revelation was what would ruin me. I'd never, never open up and trust somebody again. There was no going back after this.

Weston's eyes flashed to me, his face twisting with anguish. "Both of you, get the hell out of my apartment," he demanded. "I don't care what you have to say or who you are. Get out!"

My father shook his head violently and crossed his arms over his chest. "I'll exit when we tell my daughter everything."

"Father, leave!" I screamed, stomping my foot. I pushed off the wall, rushing to him, but was pulled back by Weston's arm wrapping around my waist.

My father snorted. "This family is poisonous, baby girl. The *entire* family," he said, bowing his head Weston's way. "Don't let him fool you, sweetheart."

"You need to handle your family matters in your own home, Parks," Mickey shouted, his upper lip curling before he bared his teeth. He looked ready to tackle my father and take a stake to his chest.

"Don't you try to leave, Mickey, or I'll make it sound so much worse without your presence," my father snarled.

"No," I cried out. I didn't want him to say it. I didn't want to relive that day.

"We have a contract," Mickey hissed.

My father chuckled. "You think I care about a contract we made nearly a decade ago?" He turned to me. "You recognize this man, don't you, baby girl?"

"No, please, please don't do this," I begged. I'd suddenly turned into the sobbing thirteen-year-old girl I'd been that day.

"Would you like me to refresh your memory?" my father asked.

"Somebody, please tell me what in the hell is going on!" Weston screamed.

"Answer the question. Do you or do you not recognize this man?" he asked again.

"You know I do," I seethed.

twenty-eight

ELISE

"Parks, don't do this," Mickey begged, scrambling for words as he held his hands up. He was begging, but his face was already full of defeat. He already knew it was over and he was about to be exposed.

People never won crossing my father.

I knew that too well.

Weston tightened his hold on me, bringing my shaking body to his side and squeezing me tight.

"You get your hands off my daughter," my father instructed.

"Don't take this out on my son," Mickey demanded. "He had nothing to do with this. This is about your out-of-control daughter who wants to ruin my life and my family." He looked at Weston. "Don't try to save your brother through her." His eyes went to me. "And you, he had no idea."

"I had no idea about what?" Weston asked and suddenly caught on. "Dad, what did you do?" He was beginning to put all the pieces together.

Mickey fell to his knees when my father pushed him

forward. "I'm so sorry. I was young and didn't know what I was doing," he cried out.

"Dad … please tell me it's not what I think it is," Weston said, scrubbing a hand up and down his face.

"You were a grown man!" I screamed, pulling out of Weston's hold to march up to Mickey. "You know exactly what you were doing, you piece of shit!"

Mickey's head was bowed down, his chin lowering to his chest. The asshole avoided all eye contact with me. I took a deep breath. I was finally facing the man who'd haunted me for years.

He was the first guy who had sex with me—the first man who had raped me—the one who'd craved to pop my cherry. I hadn't seen him since that day, but all the painful memories came back in flashes. He was winning again and making me lose myself.

And he couldn't even look at me.

Weston paced behind me, and I jumped at the sound of a picture smashing to the floor when his hand went through the drywall. "I'm trying everything—*everything*—in my power not to go over there and kill you," he told his father.

My eyes widened as I watched Weston. I'd never seen him this angry. He looked ready to beat the shit out of his father and then burn the entire building down.

Mickey hung his arms at his sides and stared at his feet. "I'm sorry, son."

"Don't apologize to me!" Weston screamed. "It's not me you need to be apologizing to." He stepped toward me and stopped at my side. "Look at her."

Mickey squeezed his eyes shut.

"I said, look at her!"

His dad opened his eyes slightly.

"Do you see her?"

Tears pooled down my face. I tried to rid myself clean of each one with the swipe of my hand.

Weston grabbed his dad's chin and jerked it up. "You hurt this girl. Those tears running down her face are because of your actions! You hurt her! She deserves more than an apology, but let's start with that. I want to see you beg her for forgiveness." He returned to me and whispered, "And I don't want you to give that to him," to me.

A few tears slipped down Mickey's cheeks, but I felt nothing. I was happy he was hurting. It was his turn for him to lose what was precious to him.

"I said, apologize!" Weston screamed. "Or I swear to God, I will pick up the phone, call every person in our family, and tell them what a pathetic, pedophiliac scumbag you are."

"I'm sorry!" Mickey yelled out. "I'm so sorry! I've regretted it for years. I didn't think. Your mom and I were having problems, and I wasn't thinking clearly."

Everyone waited for my reaction.

"I need you to leave," I said sternly.

My nails dug into Weston's hand. As good as it felt to hear Mickey grovel, his apology didn't mean anything to me. It was half-assed, half-hearted, and too late.

Mickey stood, and his eyes watered as he stared at Weston. "Please, son, don't tell your mother. It will tear our family apart."

"She deserves to know," Weston replied. "She needs to know what kind of monster you are."

"But I apologized. You said—"

"I lied," Weston yelled, cutting him off. "Just like you've been doing for years. Do you think that sad excuse of an apology makes you a better man? Do you think I'd want you around my mother? Around my sister? My niece?"

"Don't act like you're innocent in this," he argued.

Weston's hand tightened around mine.

Huh?

"What is he talking about?" I asked.

"Get out of my house," Weston demanded, ignoring me.

Mickey gestured to his son, and his face turned cold. "You tell your mother about this, and I will tell your new girlfriend about your secrets. If you cause me to lose the woman I love, I'll do the same to you." His finger moved to me. "I will tell her *everything*. Keep that in mind before you make any phone calls." With that, he turned around, and the door slammed behind him as he left.

"How did you know I was here?" I finally asked my father, who was quietly standing in the corner.

Even though this shitshow was his fault, I didn't have the energy to argue or scream at him. As much as I wanted to know what Weston's dad had been talking about, I'd question him about it later. I'd been hit with too many bombs today. All I wanted to do was go back to bed with Weston's arms around me.

"Baby girl, you know I have cameras everywhere in that building, including the lots. Did you think I wouldn't find out where you went? I know you've been seeing Weston instead of Wendy. I called his father, told him what you two were up to, but he didn't believe me, didn't believe his son would be so reckless." He looked over at Weston, who wasn't making a move. "I know how she draws men in. I don't blame you for risking everything for her."

"It's time for you to go," Weston finally said and pointed to the door. "If Elise wants to see you, she'll call. Now, get the hell out of my home."

My father whistled loudly. "Not too fast, boy. We can't just let out some of the secrets. Like I said, it's honesty hour."

"What is he talking about?" I asked Weston again, hesitation clear in my voice.

"He's convincing you to come home," Weston answered. "He'll say anything to keep you away from me and locked up in his miserable tower." He avoided eye contact with me, but his hand still held mine.

"Oh, you did that yourself, *Doctor*. Now, how did you two meet?" my father went on.

I refused to answer and stared at Weston.

"It's okay," he went on. "You don't have to tell me. We all know it was at Sun Gate. Weston was your doctor for a day, correct?"

Neither one of us said anything.

"He was concerned about what you'd told him there."

"You were?" My voice cracked, but relief fell through me. He'd tried to fight for me and give me a voice.

Weston's free hand scrubbed over his face before he moved it to press the edge of his knuckle to his lips.

"I told him it wasn't true, but he said he wanted to investigate it," my father said.

He'd believed me. He'd fought for me. I loved this man.

My father wasn't done yet. "When I realized he wasn't going to let it go, I offered him a check to keep his mouth shut. He took it. He chose money over you."

Pain hit me everywhere—my chest, throat, and heart. I'd thought Weston being Mickey's son had hurt, but it was nothing compared to Weston betraying and lying to me. Like all the other men, he'd been a coward to my father.

"Is that true?" I asked, dropping his hand and moving away from him.

"Elise, please, just let me explain," Weston choked out, reaching for me.

"Let you explain?" I repeated with disgust. "All your words, your promises, were lies. You're a fraud ... a sellout, just like the rest of them."

"I'm nothing like them," he said weakly. "I made a mistake."

He reached out to catch me when I headed toward his bedroom.

"Don't you dare touch me," I screeched, pushing him back. "You will never touch me again." I shook my head in shame. "I should've known better. You're all the same."

My father stood as a spectator to our fighting. "Get your bags, baby girl. I'll wait for you in the car and get you back to your apartment."

"Screw you," I told him, walking away from them and slamming the bedroom door.

I hurried across the room and snatched up my bag before throwing it on the bed. The sheets still smelled of sweat and our sex.

"What are you doing?" Weston asked, coming up from behind me while I shoved my things into the bag.

"I'm leaving! What the hell does it look like I'm doing?" I shouted, heading into the bathroom, grabbing my toiletries in one sweep and dropping them into the bag.

"You can't leave me," he insisted. "You can't let us go."

"Watch me." I zipped my bag and then got dressed.

"Where are you going to go? You can't go back there."

I bumped into his side to get him to move out of my way. "I don't know. I'll figure it out."

"Stay. Please stay. I don't want you out there with nowhere to go."

I shook my head. "I'm not staying here. I can't even look at you. You're a coward, just like your father."

I had to get out of there. I had to get away from him before I lost it.

He kicked the wall. "Don't ever compare me to him." He snatched my bag from me. "Stay. I'll leave."

I jerked my head back to glare at him. I could hear my heartbeat thrumming through my ears. "What?"

"I'll go stay with my sister or at a hotel until you find somewhere else to go. Stay here as long as you'd like. I'll pack a bag right now and leave. I want you to be safe. You're not going back there. Stay. I'll leave."

I eyed him in shock. "You'd do that?"

"I'll do anything to keep you safe."

I blew out a frustrated breath. "You can't just leave your apartment."

He grabbed my face in his hand as tears flowed down my cheeks. His fingers caressed my skin, brushing them away.

My savior was now a coward.

"If you want me to go, I will," he said. "I know what I did was wrong, but I had no idea. I thought you were lying. You mean more to me than any check or job. You mean everything to me. Let me show you."

I shook my head but didn't break our embrace. "I can't."

"Please, baby," he begged.

"I can't." I whimpered at the loss of his touch.

He opened the closet and began packing a bag. "You know where everything is. If you need anything, call me."

I sniffled. "I'm not calling you."

"I understand." His voice cracked. "I'll leave you my sister's number on the counter. Call her."

"No," I said, coming to my senses. "I need to go."

"Where?" His arms fell limp at his sides. "Tell me where you are going to go."

"A hotel."

"With what money? There's no way you have enough cash to be on your own right now."

"I'll figure it out."

He grabbed my bag, held it upside down, so all the contents fell onto the bed, and tossed the bag onto the floor.

"Quit it!" I scrambled while trying to pick up everything.

"You'll be safe here. I'll be gone." He grabbed my face. "You call if you need anything. If he shows up here, you call 911 or me. Don't let him in."

"You're just like him," I seethed.

"I'm nothing like him."

"But you are."

"I'll prove it to you."

He grabbed his bag, and I cried harder as I watched him leave.

When the door shut, I fell against the floor.

Weston had taken every piece of me with him and left me with nothing but a broken heart and questions.

twenty-nine

WESTON

THREE YEARS AGO

I hesitated a moment before knocking on the open door. "Hey, Bob. Do you have a sec?"

He was sitting at his desk with a pile of paperwork in front of him. Bob was the residential director at Sun Gate and the man who'd hired me. He was also the one who had given me the background information and history on Elise.

He waved me inside. "Sure, Weston."

I moved into the room, closed the door behind me, and sat down.

He shut the folder in front of him, folded his hands together, and rested them on the desk. "How are you liking it here so far?"

I nodded a few times. "It's great. My patients seem to be progressing. The staff is helpful."

"That's great. It sounds like you're getting off to a good

start. It only gets better from here." He clapped his hands. "Is there something you want to talk about?"

"Yeah. Elise Parks."

He flinched at the mention of her name, and the mood in the room shifted into uneasiness. "Ah, our little troublemaker around here. What is she rambling and lying about now?"

I'd spent the rest of the day going over the pros and cons of talking to him and telling him what she'd told me. I didn't know if Elise had been telling the truth or trying to get me on the bad side of Bob to get fired. I didn't believe this entire facility would cover up a woman being raped. It made no sense, but my conscience told me to check it out. If it was true, I was going to do everything in my power to help heal her. I wouldn't trust anything else she had to say if it was a lie.

"She told me something troubling," I told him.

"Let me guess. She told you she was raped?"

I nodded. "She did."

He rubbed his balding head. "The girl is lying, just like she had with other therapists, accusing them of sleeping with her." He shook his head. "This happens with each new counselor, but most of them have the experience to know when a patient is lying."

I shouldn't have come to him.

I opened my mouth, ready to reason with him and apologize, but he didn't give me the chance.

"That's not an insult toward you. Others have come to me with her story. I inquired into it. It's not true. I understand you want to help the troubled girl. It's your job, but I'm telling you, it's a lie."

"Are you sure? She seemed pretty adamant about it."

"She's a habitual liar." His voice was patronizing and grew harder with each word. "Do you think I'd allow something that devastating to go unnoticed with a patient of mine?"

I didn't need to get fired.

"I understand. I just want to make sure I'm helping my patients."

He laughed. "Shock factor, my friend. I told you, the girl lies. She loves the attention."

I brought myself up from the chair. "Okay, thank you." I moved toward the door to get out of there before he decided to fire me.

"Oh, and Weston?"

I looked back at Bob.

"I think I'm going to have Elise moved to another doctor. She seems to do better with females."

———

My jaw ticked under my skin when I pulled into the parking lot the next day. Bob had left me a voice mail, asking to meet him in his office first thing in the morning. My mind had immediately gone to Elise. I was positive I was about to be fired for not being able to handle her and wasting Bob's time.

I walked into his office to find him and another man talking. I had never seen the guy around before, but from his expensive suit and demeanor, I was positive he didn't work here. This job didn't pay enough to wear a three-thousand-dollar suit—unless he owned the place.

My mind scrambled. If the owner had been brought in, I was being fired.

"Hi, Weston. This is Clint Parks," Bob said when he noticed me frozen in the doorway. "He's Elise's father, and he would like to talk to you for a moment." Bob slid past me and left the room.

"How are you doing, Dr. Snyder? I understand you just got your degree. That must be exciting," Clint said, his eyes narrowing on me. His words were complimentary, but his tone was more like, *"don't mess with me, or I will ruin you."*

I gulped. "It's been a pretty interesting experience so far."

"I'm sure you'll do exceedingly well. I want to talk to you about my daughter." The guy wasn't into small talk. "I apologize for her atrocious behavior. Unfortunately, she has issues and is sick, which is why she's here. Since you're new, I feel you can't handle her, and she'll manipulate you until you lose your job."

I held my hand up. "Sir, I'm here to do my job. I wanted to look into it and—"

He cut me off. "If you investigate it, there will be hell to pay for you and her. The men she accuses are very influential, wealthy, and powerful. One of those men is myself, and I won't stand for it. I'm a very easy man to get along with, but not if you're crossing me. Now, how much?"

I blinked, trying to take in everything he'd just said. *Is he helping or threatening me?* Either way, I knew I'd lose my job if I argued or went against him.

"How much what?" I asked in confusion.

"How much do I have to pay you to keep your mouth shut?"

I took a step back. "Sir, isn't that bribery? If you're here to pay me off, does that mean it's true?"

"Absolutely not," he huffed. "It means that you sniffing around will cause more problems than me writing a check, especially when you find out it's a lie. Your reputation, Sun Gate's reputation, and mine will be made into a joke."

He pulled out a checkbook from his blazer pocket and set it down on the desk.

My eyes shot forward at his pen's click as he began filling the check out.

"Will that do?"

My eyes almost bulged out of my head when I saw the amount.

"I know you have student loans. Take the check, pay off your loans, and buy yourself something nice. Stay away from my daughter, and don't drag yourself into her mess."

I took a deep breath, gripping the check in my hand. "Okay," I said hesitantly.

He patted me on the back. "Smart man."

thirty

ELISE

I was hollow and numb.

There was no fight—*nothing*—left inside me.

Why had I fallen for him so hard?

And then, just like everything else in my life, it'd all fell apart.

I'd believed his lies, his bullshit, and allowed him to manipulate me.

He crushed my trust and heart with his bare hands.

He should've told me. I wasn't sure if it would've changed anything, but it could've. If he felt for me like he'd said, he would've been open and honest with, like he'd insisted I be with him. He should've told me about his mistake before it got exposed.

But he hadn't. He'd led me to believe he was the good guy.

Screw good guys.

I'd rather the assholes because at least they show who they are up front.

I sighed, falling back against the pillows in his guest bed. I'd taken all my things in there. I couldn't stand being in his bedroom, let alone his bed.

This was my first real breakup, which seemed a little unfair. From what I'd heard, your first heartbreak was supposed to be when you were a pimply-faced kid who had found out Bobby actually had a crush on your BFF and then you threw rocks at him on the playground.

But go figure that my first breakup had to be a full-blown, crazy situation.

The worst part was that I was internally struggling with myself to hate him. I was trying everything in my power to fill my heart with the resentment I wanted to feel. But I couldn't bring myself to hate him entirely.

Everything he'd done for me and the captivating emotions he'd made me feel were colliding with the angry ones and pulverizing them. That was the true definition of heartbreak. Your love for someone outweighed the hate, no matter what they'd done. You didn't forget the romantic gestures or the sweet words, even after they'd taken a hammer to your heart. You stood there, watching them leave, and fought with yourself not to beg them to stay.

Love was the most destructive poison you could consume.

After Weston had left, I'd waited an hour before returning to the living room and found it empty. I didn't know where everyone had gone, but I didn't care.

I contemplated calling Holly to ask if I could stay at her place but decided against it. Our friendship wasn't there anymore. She'd want to go out, and we'd get into trouble. She'd been texting me about giving Oliver another chance. It hurt to know my best friend didn't have my best interests at heart. That wasn't a true best friend.

I knew what I needed to do and that was to come up with a game plan. Crashing at Weston's couldn't last forever. He had to come home eventually, and there was no way in hell I was going to be playing roomies with him. It was time I put my big-girl panties on and get my life together. I was going to find a job and then get the hell out of Chicago. It was time I became my own savior.

"Here we go," I said, grabbing my phone and making a call.

thirty-one

ELISE

"Well, well, we meet again," the arrogant voice greeted me at the door of his office.

Vincent stood in front of me with a grin while his eyes roamed down my body. He laughed when I smacked his shoulder and then kissed my cheek.

"So, we do," I said.

He gestured for me to come in and take a seat. I eyed him when I sat down. His black suit was perfectly tailored to fit his physique. He leaned back against his desk.

Yesterday, I'd narrowed down my options and decided to go with my gut. I crossed my fingers when I dialed Vincent's number and hoped he wouldn't hang up on me. He'd happily agreed to meet me.

"You know, I was surprised when I got your call," he said, stroking his chin.

"I need a job." I wasn't in the mood for small talk. I needed to know if he'd help me or if I needed to go with plan B.

He pushed forward, his eyes not leaving me, and fell into his chair. He planted his elbow on the armrest and tapped his fist against his lips. "A job? Why wouldn't you go to your father for a job? I can guarantee the pay would be much better."

I shook my head. "If I wanted to work for him, I wouldn't be here. I want you to give me a job."

"What type of job are you interested in? What skills do you have?"

"Anything really." I had no work history, no degree, nor did I know what type of job I was interested in. All I knew was that I needed money.

"Anything?" he fired back with a smirk.

"Anything that doesn't involve your dick inside my vagina," I corrected, scrunching my forehead.

"Well, that's unfortunate." He held up a hand when I shot him a nasty grin. "I'm kidding. I don't sleep with people who work for me, but I'd probably make an exception for you."

I crossed my arms. "Are you going to help me or not?"

"You can be my personal assistant."

"Don't you already have one of those?" I asked, referring to the woman who'd shot me a glare so evil that I was afraid to walk in front of her, fearing she'd lodge a knife in my back.

"Do you need a job?"

"Yes."

"Then, quit asking questions. You start tomorrow. Eight o'clock. Don't be late."

My muscles loosened, and my lungs let out a rush of relief. *Thank God.* I was one step closer to my goal of being gone.

"Eight o'clock," I repeated before lifting myself from the chair. "I also need another favor."

He laughed. "You haven't even started yet, and you're already asking for favors?"

"I need an advance."

"You need an advance?" He said each word slowly.

"Yes. I need new clothes." I threw my hands down my body. I was wearing a pair of jeans and a T-shirt. I didn't want to go home and get clothes, so I'd worked with what I'd packed when I fled my apartment. "Obviously, I can't wear this."

He gazed at me with focus and shook his head. "I'm not even going to ask." He opened a drawer and handed me five crisp hundred-dollar bills. "Don't you stand me up."

"I'll be here." I turned to leave but paused before I made it to the door and peeked at him over my shoulder. "And Vincent?"

He raised a brow. "Yeah?"

I smiled. "Thank you."

He winked. "I got you, girl."

thirty-two

ELISE

I glanced up from my ice cream bowl at the sound of someone unlocking the front door. I shut my eyes, counted to ten, and opened them back up to find a petite, dark-haired girl walking in with an armful of grocery bags that covered half her face.

"Here, let me help you with that," I said, dropping my spoon in the bowl, placing it on the table, and getting up.

"Thanks," she said, handing over a bag, and I carefully set it down on the counter.

Weston had sent me a text earlier, saying his sister was coming over to grab some more of his clothes and drop off some things.

"Hi," the girl said, wiping her bangs away from her forehead before pushing her arm out my way. "I'm Julia, Weston's sister."

I blinked a few times and dragged my hand out to shake hers. There was no mistaking that the two were related. Her brown hair, the same color as his, was cut at the peak of her shoulders, and blunt bangs were cut diagonally across her forehead. Her skin was makeup-free, and she didn't have a blemish in sight.

"Hi," I squeaked out, wringing my hands together.

Did Weston tell her about me? Of course, he had, or she wouldn't be here. I was curious as to how much she knew and if she was aware her father had raped me.

She started pulling groceries out. "He was right. You are gorgeous."

I blushed, and she started loading groceries into the fridge.

Goddammit!

I didn't want his compliment to make me happy, but it did. The fact that Weston had been complimenting me to his family made me feel all warm and fuzzy inside.

Damn you, heart. It would be best if you remembered we hate him. He crushed us.

"Thank you," I said shyly, not sure what else to say. It would've been weird for me to tell her to relay the message of *kiss my ass* to her brother.

We quietly unloaded the rest of the groceries.

"Okay, do you need anything else?" Julia asked.

"No, I think I'm good," I replied. "Tell Weston I should be out in the next week or two."

"I'll let him know, but there's no rush." She dropped money on the counter. "He said you like Chinese takeout and you'd probably need an egg-roll fix soon."

Hell no, I wasn't going to allow him to worm his way back into my heart with Chinese food.

"I don't want his money." I snatched up the bills, tried to hand it back to her, but she held her hands up.

"I know what my father did to you," she said out of nowhere, startling me.

I fell back against the counter. Her eyes were dead set on mine, making it more difficult for me to hide my humiliation.

"What?" I asked in shock. *Why was she bringing this up?*

"Weston told me. None of this is your fault, you know that, right?"

I glanced down at the tiled floor, scraping my sock-covered feet against it before gaining the courage to stare at her.

"Look," I said, my voice turning harsh, "I appreciate you wanting to reach out, but I'm not a fan of talking to strangers, especially given who your family is."

"I understand," she said gently. "If you do decide you ever want to talk, I know Weston left you my number. Call me. I promise I won't say anything to him about you reaching out."

"Thanks. I'll keep that in mind."

"And one more thing."

I blew out an exasperated breath. I wanted her gone.

"I know my brother hurt you but give him a chance to explain himself. I've never seen him so distraught. His intention was never to hurt you. He loves you and was trying to protect you. My brother is a good person, one of the best men I know. He was put in a tough situation and wasn't sure what to do about it."

He loves you. Her words seared into my brain, rushing down to bite my heart.

No, he didn't love me. You didn't hide something that serious from someone you loved.

"I know you care about your brother and don't want to see him hurting, but I can't do that. I can't see him," I answered, slamming my eyes shut and praying to God I wouldn't cry in front of her. "I can't do it."

thirty-three

ELISE

"You ever going to tell me what's going on with you and your dad?" Vincent asked, propping his feet up on his desk, his emerald eyes searching mine from across his office. His hair was freshly cut and combed to the side.

I swore the guy had more hair appointments than I did. Actually, I knew he did because, apparently, it was in my *job description* to accompany him to each one.

"Nothing to tell," I muttered, dragging my attention toward the floor to mask the hatred sparking inside me at the mention of him.

It was week four of working for Vincent— -or *with* Vincent, considering I'd been by his side almost every minute of the day. The man wouldn't let me out of his sight. I was his assistant, dining companion, and shopping partner. I'd spent more time with him than with anyone else in my life.

I hung out in his office or ran simple errands when he went to meetings. He told me I had to work my way up when I asked for more responsibilities. But I knew it was because there were

199

no open positions. He'd given me the job because he wanted me there and probably felt sorry for me. I didn't care. I'd take a sympathy job if it made me money.

I hadn't heard from Weston or my father. I'd bought a new phone and changed my number with my first paycheck. Then, I had gone apartment hunting, laid down a deposit on the second place I was shown, and moved out of Weston's apartment the same day.

Staying there had been killing me. Reminders of us were everywhere. I'd spent the following week sleeping on an air mattress until my next payday. Vincent was paying me well, most likely more than any typical assistant.

"Oh, come on," he replied, clacking a pen against his teeth. "You're Elise Parks. Everyone in this city knows who you are and your story. Your dad has controlled every aspect of your life since you were born. He's ruled you with an iron fist. You'd go out, raise havoc, and then disappear for a few weeks. Then, the process would repeat. Now, suddenly, you're out on your own with no personal driver, no money, and no place to live. It doesn't add up."

I shot him an annoyed glare, causing him to laugh again. "I'm a grown woman. It was time I finally went out on my own," I answered.

A boyish grin spread across his face. "Ahh ... I see. You've blossomed and grown your wings. Fly, little butterfly. Fly."

I rolled my eyes as he dropped his feet, getting comfortable in the red leather chair.

His office was professional but eclectic at the same time. Instead of going for the typical black furniture, everything was bright red. Sophisticated photos of nude women paintings and his degrees hung on the walls.

He whistled, pointing a finger my way. "But now, it's time for a favor, my little butterfly. I need something from you."

"What?" I asked skeptically, drawing in a brow.

"A date."

I held my hand up, stopping him from saying anything more. "Hell no. We've already had this conversation. I'm not sleeping with you, Peterson."

He grinned in amusement. "Yet," he fired back. "You're not sleeping with me yet."

He was convinced I'd eventually land in his bed. There was no way any woman had ever said no to him. He was sexy, successful, wealthy, and a smooth talker. He could make a girl wet with just one sentence.

But Weston had ruined me. The asshole that I was still in love with had wrecked me. There was no way I would be able to sleep with Vincent without thinking of Weston. I couldn't even stand the thought of someone else's hands touching me, let alone let them stick their dick inside me. I was trying my hardest to fall out of love with him, but I hadn't found the solution or the strength to do it yet.

"I'm not sleeping with you *ever*," I corrected.

"We'll see, darling. Saturday night, you're mine."

"Are you going to tell me where we're going?" I asked, tapping one of my new heels against the plush gray carpet.

Vincent had done a lot for me. If he hadn't given me a job, I would've either still been at Weston's place, back at my father's, or at some homeless shelter in the city. I couldn't tell him no. He was the only reason I was standing on my own two feet.

"The Field Museum. They're having a charity event my parents attend every year, and they're insisting I go." He shook his head. "I hate those things, so I need a date to keep me company."

"Seems easy enough. Sure."

He leaned back in his chair. "Oh, and they're under the assumption we're a couple."

My head jerked back, and I wanted to smack the stupid grin off his face. "You told them we're dating?"

"I didn't tell them anything. They assume we're dating, and I haven't corrected them."

"Why would they assume we're dating?"

"Haven't you been reading any of the city's blogs?"

"Uh, no." I hated gossip and anything that had to do with it. At seventeen, I'd stopped reading the blogs when one did a false special on me, writing that I had contracted almost every sexually transmitted disease known to man.

"We're labeled the city's new *it* couple."

"You'd better rectify that."

"Please, it's just one night. I don't see what's so wrong with dating me. I like to think I'm a pretty good catch. It will be like hanging out, just like we have been."

"Will my father be there?" If he was, there was no way in hell I was going.

He shrugged. "Not sure. The guest list is huge, so I doubt you'll even see him if he is."

"Fine," I groaned. "But if I see him, I'm gone."

"I'll tell my parents we have to go because you need some cock."

"Do you want me to change my mind?"

"Got it. If we see him, we go. It would be easier to understand if you just told me what he did."

I gulped. "Nope."

Weston was the only man I'd ever let know everything. Which sucked because if I ever did get into another relationship, I'd never be able to give them all of me, like I had him. You could only give everything you had to one person. Once you'd released all that you are to someone, you're hollowed out. You could never be reconstructed to hand over that part of you again.

He pulled himself up from his chair, walked to the closet, and withdrew a wrapped box with a bright red bow on top.

"Elise Parks, one of these days, I will figure you out, and you'll see I'm not such a bad guy. Sooner or later, you're going to let me in." He handed me the box.

I instantly recognized the Saks Fifth Avenue box. He'd bought me a few gifts to update my wardrobe since I didn't have much.

"I wouldn't bet on it."

He sighed, shaking his head. "Saturday night. I'll be at your place at eight."

thirty-four

ELISE

I puckered my ruby-red lips before smacking them together. "Oh, MAC, how I missed thee," I cooed into the mirror. I parted my lips, swiped some more color on, and smacked them together again.

I reached up and smoothed down my curls. My eyelids were painted a light gold with winged eyeliner coming off each side.

I settled my gaze on my reflection. I was headed down the road of happiness. I didn't fully love myself yet, but I was getting there. I was no longer the reigning princess of the Parks' empire. The girl portrayed as the oversexed bitch was gone. I was now a girl discovering herself without another dictating how she was doing it. I was finally free.

"Be good, be safe, and only spread your legs if he's wearing a Rolex around his wrist," Carrie, the girl who lived across the hall, advised, collapsing onto my bed with a glass of wine in her hand.

"Careful. I just bought those sheets," I scolded.

She held her drink up in the air, rolling her eyes. "Happy now?"

I nodded.

"And don't forget to take my advice."

"Seriously? Advice? What kind of advice is that?" I asked, dousing my strands with hair spray.

"One from a hooker," she replied with no shame.

The first night I'd moved in, Carrie had shown up at my doorstep with a bottle of wine in her hand. She had taken one glance at my bare apartment, grabbed my hand, and then had me watching TV at her place.

She was twenty-six and gorgeous. Her ruby-red hair was pulled back around her crown with loose waves flowing to the sides, framing her flawless face. Her married boyfriend paid for her apartment, so he could make his four-times-a-week visit to her and get laid.

Like me, she didn't believe in love. That might've been why we clicked so easily. She claimed it was a bullshit fairy tale parents told their daughters, so they'd wait for a Prince Charming and not give it up to the first boy who smiled their way. She'd slept with so many men who had made vows to their women, promising to cherish them in their marriage, and then would sneak over to sleep with her.

"You're not a hooker," I threw back, resulting in an arched brow from her. "Okay, you're not a straight out-of-the-box hooker," I corrected, and she busted out in laughter.

I'd technically been a hooker myself. I'd put out for business deals. Carrie put out for a place to live and Chanel bags. Everyone put out for something. Some just didn't know it yet.

She pointed my way, her lips forming a smile. "*Au contraire,* I'm a *high-end* hooker. Does that make it sound better? Does that give me a little bit of morality?"

"You're a home-wrecker. A side chick. He takes care of you

like any guy would take care of a girlfriend or wife. It's not like he pays you by the hour, has you blow him, and then leaves you at some cheap motel with a bad case of the clap."

I didn't exactly agree with Carrie sleeping with married men. I personally would never be the other woman, but to each their own. She had her own problems to work through, and I wasn't one to judge. She'd been a good friend to me.

"You're right," she said, her voice perking up. "So, next time I have an angry wife coming over to smash my face in with a golf club, I'm going to send them your way, so you can reason with them."

"What? Has that happened?"

"More times than you'd think."

I rose from my vanity chair to grab the box Vincent had given me from my closet. I should've opened it earlier to make sure whatever was in there fit, but I didn't know if I was going to bail or not. Then, Carrie had come over, insisting I needed to go out, and I'd caved.

She jumped up from my bed when I set the box down on my sheets and opened it. "Girl, this dress is perfect," she said as I carefully spread the dress out on my bed.

We both stood to the side, admiring it. The floor-length black dress was stunning. Delicate beading spread down the chest and sides. The back was completely bare, and the silk lace bunched together at the base of the spine.

"Damn, the boy has taste," she said, reaching for the tag. "And Gucci. I like him for you. You should have his babies." She laughed when I smacked her shoulder.

Carrie was right. Vincent was being the perfect gentleman with me. But he wanted something I couldn't give him. Not to mention, I still wasn't completely trusting. I didn't know if he saw me as a game and would drop me after I gave it up to him.

He was a playboy, and playboys didn't get their reputations for having long-term relationships.

I untied my robe, and Carrie helped me slip into the dress.

"By the way, what's going on with him?" she asked, zipping me up.

I shrugged, clasping a bracelet around my wrist. "Nothing."

"Girl, he's hot as hell. I don't understand why you won't give him a chance. You have to move on sooner or later. The best way to get over a guy is to get under someone else. I know you loved Weston, but you can't just give up on men. A girl has to get laid sooner or later."

One night, I'd drunkenly confessed to her how Weston had broken my heart. She didn't know everything—just that he'd left me completely broken.

"And I have a feeling he's going to want to get under you tonight," she said, turning me around to look in the floor-length mirror.

My hand flew to my mouth. The dress wasn't provocative or immature.

It was sexy but classy.

I felt beautiful.

"Every man in that place will be salivating over you."

I laughed. "Yeah, right. Not the ones who know my rep."

She took a swig of wine. "Guys don't care about a girl's rep. They only care about her bra size and how many dates it takes to get inside her panties. And girls only care about other women's reps because they're intimidated by them."

My vanity vibrated as my phone rang. Carrie picked it up before I had the chance to.

"It's Vincent. He's on his way up," she said when she hung up. She grinned and jumped up in the air. "Go have fun, girl."

thirty-five

ELISE

"You look stunning," Vincent said before loudly whistling when I opened my front door.

He kissed me on the cheek and led me down the stairs to the black limousine waiting outside.

Vincent looked just as good. He wore a tailored black suit with a black bow tie. Girls were going to be fighting me to go home with my date.

"Thank you," I said, feeling shy as I ran my hand over my dress. "I love it."

He stopped his driver from opening the limousine door for me. "Rodney, stay. I got this."

Rodney—a tall, older man—nodded his head and got back in the car.

Vincent opened the door, allowing me to slide in, and scooted in behind me.

"Thank you for the dress. I know it's expensive," I said, settling in my seat.

His face went soft. "You deserve it, babe."

I jerked when he scooted closer, the warmth of his hand spreading over mine.

"God, this is going to make me sound like such a pussy," he groaned, running a hand through his hair.

I stared at him in confusion.

"I know you've been going through some shit, and you won't tell me what, but I hope, eventually, you will. But I like you. I mean, I like you—like you."

I let out a fake laugh, trying to make light of the situation. Vincent had been a good friend to me. I didn't want to hurt him. I knew what it felt like to have someone hurt you.

"Do you say that to every girl you get in the back of your limo?" I asked jokingly.

He chuckled. "Eh ... I don't usually do much talking in here."

I had to give him credit for being honest. I glanced around the ten-seater, wrinkling my nose. "Gross. Should I be sitting somewhere else, like up there with the driver, so I don't get yours or anyone else's bodily fluids on me?"

He threw his head back. "You don't have to worry about that. I get it professionally cleaned after each use." He scratched his head. "I'll give you time, babe. I know you need it but know I'm here for you if you need anything. If you want to talk, if you need a friend, anything."

I sighed. "Are you saying that because you really care, or because you want to sleep with me?"

"You want me to be honest?"

"Of course, I want you to be honest."

"I'd say fifty-fifty. I care about you, but I'd love to get into those panties too. I can only imagine how good it would feel to be inside you." He studied our hands, and I could feel mine slowly start to sweat. "And someone likes dirty talk," he went on, grinning wide and squeezing my hand. "I'll keep that in mind for when the day comes."

I groaned, shoving his side playfully. "God, you are just so ..."

"Sexy?"

"No."

"Irresistible?"

"No ... crazy."

I blushed when he grabbed my face to massage my cheeks gently. He peered at my red lips, mesmerized, before moving forward and brushing his lips against them.

"I know you feel something for me, and I'll wait until you realize it yourself," he whispered against them, kissing me again and then pulling away.

I ran my fingers over my lips in shock. *Why didn't I stop him? Why didn't I slap him?* I wasn't sure. I wasn't sure of anything anymore, but maybe hanging out with Vincent wasn't so bad at that moment.

"You think on that," he continued, opening the door when we pulled up in front of the museum. "Stay by my side, and if you want to leave, I got you, babe." He grabbed my hand and walked me up the steps to the entrance.

I scanned the area when we walked in, my stomach twisting. My heart thudded against my chest as Vincent guided me through the packed crowd.

"Would you like something to eat or drink?" he asked, his hand still in mine.

"Sure. I need to use the restroom really quick though," I replied, still inspecting the room for *him*. I wanted to do a survey of the premises before I got comfortable, making sure no one was there that I didn't want to see.

"You want me to come with you?"

He frowned when I shook my head.

"I'll be fine."

I crept shyly along the outside of the crowd toward the

restroom and then slammed the stall door shut when I got there. I needed a few minutes to myself before having a conversation with anyone. I was sure Vincent wanted to introduce me to his parents.

When I walked out of the stall, there were women staring in the mirror and touching up their makeup. They stared at me in disgust when I walked to the sink to wash my hands.

They knew who I was.

And they didn't like me being there.

I ignored them. These women were the least of my problems right now.

"I can't believe he came here with you," one blonde spat angrily.

"Yeah, I know," another woman agreed. "Vincent can do so much better, but he's probably just using her like every other guy does."

"Well, believe it," I said, giving them a sarcastic smile. I didn't have time for their jealous bullshit. I had bigger problems on my plate. "And he obviously wasn't satisfied with you, considering you're in here, whining about it in the restroom, and I'm the one by his side."

I turned around and left the restroom, ignoring their nasty insults at my back. I snatched a flute of champagne from a server on my way back to Vincent.

But I didn't make it that far.

"I didn't expect to see you here."

I stopped dead in my tracks. Panic rose through me, and I almost dropped my drink at the voice coming from behind me.

thirty-six

WESTON

I wasn't sure if she'd be at the event, but I'd hoped she would. I'd watched her, followed every story that mentioned her, and I wanted to throw my computer every time I saw a mention of her with Vincent.

What the hell was she doing with him?

There were talks of them dating, but I knew Elise. They weren't dating. The stupid blogs had no evidence of that either—just with them hanging out. No handholding, or kissing, and Elise sure as hell didn't look at him like she had at me when we were together.

Elise's back tensed at my voice. I held in a breath, waiting for her to turn around. We were so close that I could stretch my arm and run my fingers along her skin. But I was too nervous to try—fearing her reaction. I wasn't allowed to touch her. She wasn't mine anymore.

She pretended not to hear me, like I was invisible, in hopes I'd take the clue, back away, and leave.

Well, that wasn't happening.

I drank in the smooth contours of her body in the formfitting dress that hugged tight to every one of her perfect curves. Her dark mane was down, hanging loose around her shoulders in curls. This beautiful woman had once been mine, and I missed her. I needed her back in my arms, in my life, because she was still in my heart.

"Look at me, please," I begged, blocking out the music and conversations of those around us.

They faded out—my only focus on her.

It was just the two of us.

She had to hear me out, and I would do everything I could to convince her to. I'd beg. I'd drop to my knees and grovel for her forgiveness in front of the room. I'd throw out my pride, masculinity, anything, if it meant she'd come back to me.

Another minute passed.

Nothing.

I was losing hope.

"Please," I continued to beg.

"I'd rather not," she replied sharply. "I have nothing to say to you."

"You don't have to say anything. Let me do the talking."

This was my only chance. I didn't know if I'd have this opportunity again.

My heart burned when she swung around to face me, and my stomach knotted when our eyes met. She scowled at me in hate—categorizing me into the lists of all the other men who'd wronged her. That hurt so damn much.

I cleared my throat, struggling for the perfect words to convey the deep regret inside me. They had to be good enough, or she'd never forgive me.

"There you are. I thought you'd bailed on me.

Another strike against me.

I clenched my jaw when Wendy came to my side and looped her arm through mine.

Not good.

Finally, I got the opportunity to speak with Elise, and it backfired in my face. The urge to flick Wendy off my arm like she was an unwanted fly ate at me, but I wasn't that type of man. So, I slid my arm out of hers without paying her a glance.

Elise held all my attention. She'd straightened her stance at Wendy's presence and glared at her.

"Oh, hi, Elise," Wendy greeted, noticing the face-off between us.

Elise downed the rest of her drink. "Hey, Wendy."

I coughed, hoping Wendy would get the hint that this wasn't a good time. Thankfully, Wendy was smart.

She clapped her hands. "I'm going to go check on your mom or ... do something." She shot me an uneasy smile and rushed off.

Elise's face reddened, matching the hue of her lipstick. "You sure moved on pretty quick, huh?" She shook her head, grabbing another glass of champagne from a server walking by. "Were you two dating the entire time you were playing me?"

"Playing you?" I repeated, rubbing the back of my neck roughly.

She didn't say anything.

"Wendy and I are nothing. I'm only here for my mom." *And you.* "My mother is divorcing my dad and struggling with adjusting to life on her own. As bad as I wanted to skip this event, I didn't want to let her down. She needs to forget my scumbag father."

I winced, a bitter taste forming in my mouth.

I hated even calling him my father.

He was a disgrace.

"You came here for your mother, but you brought a date?" she sneered.

Wendy wasn't my date. She and my mother had known each other for decades, so she brought my mother to the event, and I met them. She wasn't there on my account.

"And what do you call being here with Vincent? *A date?*" I fired back. Saliva built up in the back of my throat.

The thought of Vincent's—or anyone's—hands on her made me sick to my stomach.

Of anyone else helping her through her struggles and trauma.

She chewed on her lower lip. "Not that it's any of your business, but Vincent and I are just friends."

"Same thing with Wendy and me." I lowered my voice and wearily took a step closer. "Do you know *he's* here?"

She hung her head low. I could tell she wanted to look around for him, but she was either too scared or didn't want me to know she cared. "I didn't."

I'd noticed the bastard the second I walked in. Her father was keeping his distance, but I knew he had seen me. I wasn't sure if he knew Elise was there, but I didn't want him finding out and coming near her.

"If you want to go, we can," I said.

"*We can go?*" She crossed her arms and lifted her chin. "Is that your plan to get me to leave with you?" A huff released from her chest. "Using my weakness for your gain."

I exhaled a breath, throwing my arms out to my sides. "Do you think I'd do something like that?" I tapped my chest with my finger harshly. "You know I never used you." And it angered me that she'd even say something like that.

"I don't know that. I feel like I don't even know who you are. You sold yourself out to my deadbeat father, so pardon me if I refuse to believe a word that comes out of your mouth now."

I shut my eyes for a moment. "Everything I've told you—every-goddamn-thing—has been the truth. If you'd let me explain—"

She grew angrier. "Omission is the same as lying."

"I planned to tell you."

"Then, why didn't you?"

"I wanted to wait."

"Wait until when?"

My voice turned soft. "Until you loved me enough."

She flinched, my words hitting her like a ton of bricks. "What does that even mean?" she cried out, grabbing the attention of people around us but she didn't care. She took a step forward, stabbing a finger into my chest. "Don't you dare try that psychological bullshit on me."

"I wanted you to be completely in love with me—to have your love and trust—so you'd understand why I'd made that stupid decision. I made a mistake years ago that I regret so deeply that it haunts me every night. I was waiting for you to love me as much as I love you." My heart pounded against my chest at my admission.

Her mouth fell open, all the color draining from her face, and she shuffled back a few steps. "There's no love here."

"I know you were in love with me." I took another deep breath of courage. "I know you're still in love with me." My second declaration was risky.

"Then, why? Why didn't you tell me?"

I was right.

I could tell by her eyes. She loved me, and our being apart still hadn't changed that. Even after everything that had happened, she still loved me.

"I knew you were in love with me, but I didn't know how much reach I had inside your heart. You were still healing from all the wounds caused by your father. I wanted you to know me better, so you wouldn't think I was like him."

"But you are."

I shook my head. "I'm nothing like him." I took a step forward to replace the one she'd taken away from me.

"Sure fooled me."

I took another step with precaution, waiting for her reaction, but she didn't move away. "I would never purposely hurt you. I've risked for you. I've risked my career, my family, everything for you. And I'd do it again in a heartbeat. I'd choose you over everything and everyone."

"If you had to risk everything for me, then obviously, we're no good for each other."

"You come first. I can always find another job. I can start over. If I have you by my side, I can make everything right in my life."

"I thought you'd gotten lost in the restroom," Vincent said, approaching her.

Great. Now, her date was interrupting us. *Why the hell did either of us even have dates?*

My face melted in horror when his arm curled around her waist, and he tugged her into his side. Elise didn't pull away from him, but she didn't move any closer either. I wanted to slap his hand off her.

"I ran into an old friend," Elise said with a sarcastic smile.

"Oh, hey, Weston. What's going on?" Vincent smacked my back. "I haven't seen you around in ages."

I knew Vincent. We'd attended the same private school together.

I scratched my neck. "Yeah, I kind of left this world behind me."

"I don't blame you." He signaled to Elise and me with his chin. "How do you two know each other?"

"We met through my father," Elise quickly answered.

"Actually, we dated," I corrected, clenching my teeth and glaring at Vincent.

I had nothing against him personally, but when it came to the woman I loved, I had a problem with anyone who interfered.

Vincent released his hold from Elise, obviously getting the point. "Seriously?" he asked in shock. "You two?"

"We didn't exactly date," Elise said. "We went out a few times."

I shook my head. "No, we definitely dated. Pretty much lived together too."

"All right," Vincent drew out, clearly uncomfortable and not sure what to do next. He liked her but was contemplating whether he wanted to fight for her.

"And we're in *love*," I added with a punch, stressing the last word, glaring at him to make my warning clear.

Vincent smirked. "I get it. I get it." He nodded his head toward me. "You two obviously have some shit to work out. I could compete with you anytime for a woman, Snyder, but not when it comes to love. Love makes people crazy."

He whispered something into Elise's ear, causing her to nod, and then drew a finger toward me. "If you piss her off and she wants to leave, I'm taking her."

"That won't be happening," I replied, an edge to my tone.

Vincent whistled before walking away. Elise could've left with him, but she hadn't. That gave me some hope.

"Was that necessary?" she snapped.

I shrugged. "People need to know you're off the market."

She tossed her hands in the air, champagne splashing from her glass. "News flash: I am on the market."

"How can you be on the market when you're mine?"

"I'm not yours," she said with a huff. "I belong to nobody."

Shit, those weren't the best words to use.

"You're right. I don't *own* you. I own *your heart.* You know it's true, so good luck trying to give it to someone else because it knows who it belongs to. Your brain might try to think something different. It might try to tell you that you've moved on from me, but it all comes down to your heart. And that, my love, is mine." I grinned wide. "But don't worry. You have mine too."

She bit into her cheek. "You need to stop saying things like that."

"I need to stop being honest?"

"Please." Her hand splayed out in front of me. "Just stop."

"Leave with me. We'll figure this out. At least give me the chance to explain myself."

I needed to figure out how to get her the hell out of there for two reasons. The first was that her father was lingering around, and I was sure he'd spot her through the crowd. I didn't want him getting to her. The second was that this was the wrong place to talk. We needed our privacy.

"Shit," I hissed, spotting Clint coming our way over Elise's shoulder. I grabbed her arm and pulled her through the crowd, ignoring her protests.

She jerked away, smacking at my arm to pull away from my hold, but I didn't let up. I pushed through a door, and we landed in an empty room.

"What the hell is wrong with you?" she shrieked, yanking away from me.

"Text Vincent. Tell him you're leaving," I demanded.

She looked close to punching me in the face. "Absolutely not. I can't just leave my date. Are you crazy?"

I pulled my phone from my pocket. "Hey, Wendy," I said to the speaker, and Elise glared at me. "Find Vincent Peterson. Tell him you're his new date." I hung up.

She threw her arms up. "Well, that's just great. Let's just hand every man interested in me over to Wendy."

I couldn't hold back my chuckle, resulting in another glare. "Come on. We're leaving."

"No."

I paced in front of her. "He's here." I smacked my hand against the wall. "So, you have three options: we can confront him, wait for him to confront you, or leave. As much as you probably don't want any of those options to happen tonight, one will. I'm here to support you in whatever decision you make, but he saw you and was heading straight in our direction."

She darted toward the door. I'd prepped myself to stop her from running. She jiggled the doorknob and twisted the lock instead of opening it.

"I'm not leaving with you. I'm going to call Vincent and tell him to come get me. Then, I'll leave with him."

"You're not leaving with Vincent."

"I am."

I unlocked the door, snagged her hand again, and weaved through people to go outside. She calmed down, not fighting me off to avoid making a scene. She stomped her heels down the steps, keeping up with me, and I handed the valet my parking ticket.

"I'm not getting in your car," she said while we waited, her cheeks flaming with anger underneath the moonlight.

"Yes, you are."

Again, her actions weren't matching her words. She could've easily gone back inside but stayed with me. She was conflicted, but there was still a chance. Her emotions for me were still alive and kicking, and she hated herself for it. I studied human behavior. I knew how it worked. Emotions always beat out the brain.

Always.

She crossed her arms. "Fine, but you're taking me home."

I nodded, ignoring the curious glances from the patrons around us. "I will."

"And I mean it."

The valet handed over my keys, and I tipped him. I opened the door and waited for Elise to get into the car before doing the same. She leaned forward and turned the radio on blast as I pulled out of the parking lot.

"I told you to take me home!" she shrieked when I turned down a street that wasn't hers.

I pulled into the parking garage. "I am."

"This is not my home."

"This is your home." I got out, pulled her door open, and waited for her to get out on her own—to walk upstairs and come home.

"I hate you," she spat, shooting me a cold glare as she stepped out.

thirty-seven

WESTON

Elise held up her dress, so that it wouldn't touch the ground, and said she hated me with each step up the stairs. I trailed behind her and matched every one of her flying insults with an, "I know."

When she reached our apartment, she sighed, opened her clutch, and fished out a key chain. I smirked like I'd hit the lottery while watching her cram the key into the lock.

She'd kept it.

I prayed it was because she knew we still had a chance. Not because she had been discreetly planning to come in one night and kill me in my sleep.

"I hate you," she repeated, flipping on the lights and tossing her clutch across the room.

I snagged her key from the lock while she faced me.

"I hate you, you sellout, lying asshole," she choked out, her tone filled with hurt.

This wasn't going as planned.

I blew out a pained breath. "No, you don't." I slammed the

door shut. "So, please, quit saying it to convince yourself otherwise."

I strode toward her, erasing the distance between us, and caressed the silk of her dress before curling my hands around her waist. She peered up at me, her breath faltering while she awaited my next action. She didn't move—didn't fight off my touch.

"I hate you," she whispered, her lips parting.

I sighed, inhaling her sweet perfume, and lowered my face to the curve of her neck. She pressed her body into mine as I rained kisses along her soft skin.

I should pull away.

We need to talk.

She needed to hear me out, but I froze when I opened my mouth to tell her that.

I drew away from her, and her teeth tugged on the edge of my lower lip. Her eyes smoldered. I shuddered when she reached out and brushed her hand along my arm.

My heart surged in my chest, and I slid my hands down to her ass, gripping it firmly.

"Then, fuck me like you do," I whispered, our mouths only inches apart.

Her eyes came alive. My response had taken her aback, but she didn't unblind us. Those words doused her like propane, and my touch ignited the fire already burning deep inside her. Her hands smacked into my chest before she slid a single finger along the opening. The sound of her ripping my shirt down the middle, buttons scattering along the floor, interrupted the quiet air. I shivered, her palms planting on my bare chest, and she pushed me backward until my back bumped into the wall.

She gripped my wrists, dragging my arms up and pinning them above my head. I threw my head back in ecstasy at the feel of her teeth tugging on a nipple.

"I hate you so much," she muttered against my flesh.

I shuddered, my entire body convulsing at the feel of her tongue licking me down. She fell to her knees but was careful not to mess up her dress. She played with the buckle of my pants, and with a snap, they fell to the floor. Within seconds, her hand wrapped around my cock.

No teasing touches, no buildup, just straight to my aching dick.

"Do you want to talk?" I asked like an idiot. I wanted her mouth around my cock, but she couldn't do that if we were talking.

"If I wanted to talk, I wouldn't have my hand wrapped around your cock," she said, her eyes devious.

I jerked against the wall when her mouth met my cock. She licked her tongue down my length. I braced myself, feeling her take me over with only the power of her tongue.

I tilted my hips forward, meeting her while she took me in her warm and willing mouth. I jumped, my cock pulsating when she reached for my balls, massaging them. I pumped in and out of her mouth, maintaining a nice rhythm, until she halted. I huffed, peering down at her when I fell from her sweet lips.

"Come on," she said, grabbing my legs in assistance to push herself up.

I gulped, tugging my pants back up my waist and obeying her command as she led me into the bedroom. I was letting her call the shots. I was bowing to her pussy tonight, allowing her to make the rules. She could act like she hated me, loved me, or wanted to kill me, and I'd take it all from her.

"Let me get this, baby," I said, smoothing my hands over her shoulder before unzipping her dress.

I watched it slide down her body, inch by inch, until it hit her feet. Then, I helped her out of it. As she stood before me, I licked my lips, taking her in wearing only a bra, panties, and heels.

I collapsed onto my knees, gripping her leg, and easing her foot onto the bed. I ran my thumb between the lace of her panties before brushing them to the side. She took a deep breath when I slipped two fingers inside her soaked center. She was so drenched that I felt her dripping down my fingers—her juices hitting my wrist.

My heart raged in my chest as I spread her legs wider. She groaned out curses when I pulled my fingers out of her pussy and lowered my face to her soft folds. I started with one easy lick, upping my pace when she gasped, and held her wobbly leg in place. I grinned against her pussy, my tongue driving wildly inside her, and slapped her ass before grabbing a handful of it to bring her closer to my mouth.

"Don't stop," she muttered, rotating her hips and melting against my tongue.

I wanted to consume every piece of her, feel her come apart on my tongue, in my mouth, and that was exactly what she did. She moaned out that she hated me again before coming undone.

I lathered up the excess juices trickling down her thighs, massaging her ass, and pulled away to level my gaze on her.

"Do you still hate me?" I asked, giving her a hopeful smile before teasingly licking my bottom lip.

I wished I could read her mind, but she wasn't giving anything away, except that she was turned on.

Her eyes were glazed over as she stared at me intensely. "It depends," she said, a sly smile spreading over her full lips.

"On?" I asked.

"On whether or not you let me ride your cock."

Is that even a question I had to consider?

"Whatever you want, love. I'm all yours."

Smiling, she jerked out of my hold and scooted backward on the bed. I trailed behind her on my hands and knees, kissing her lips when I reached her. She devoured my mouth like she was losing oxygen and I was the tank reviving her.

"Pants off," she demanded, cupping my hard and ready cock.

I kicked off my shoes, dragging my pants off behind them.

"And you're still excited for me?"

"Always," I said, lifting her chin to kiss her again. "Always for you." I tugged her panties off, ripping them in the process, and threw them across the room.

I exhaled when she pushed me down on my back and straddled my lap. She lifted, grabbing my cock and dragging it through her warmth before slamming down on me.

My back arched, coming off the bed, at the feel of her taking in every inch of me. I moaned, a fist going to my mouth, my other hand latching on to her hip. She moved fast, riding me hard. Our bodies slammed together, our skin slapping against each other's while our groans and sighs filled the bedroom.

"Your bra off," I groaned, flexing my hips to meet her every stroke. The room was burning up, my head going hazy while I struggled to gain my breath. I'd missed this.

She unclasped her bra and tossed it across the room. I watched her breasts bounce with each grind. I felt powerless underneath her as she rode me hard, finally falling to rest her hands on my chest, her nipples within mouth's reach. I lifted my head to suck one. She gave me a faint smile and slowed her pace as she fed her breast to me—allowing me to suck hard. Her stomach slid against mine as she kept riding me. My dick hit every inch of her.

So much was going on—so many emotions, sensations, feelings. I was ready to bust inside her.

"Are you almost there?" she asked, riding me harder. She

was taking her frustrations out on me, like she had those other men.

I gripped her hips so she couldn't move. "I will not be one of those guys," I said, meeting her eyes.

She shook her head, her voice strained. "You'll never be one of those guys." Her hips bucked, begging for release so she could move, but I didn't.

"Tell me you love me."

Her face squished up, appearing combative and then turning soft. "I love you," she whispered.

I pulled my hands away, releasing her, and she slammed back down on me. And it was like her declaration had set us both off. She spasmed, coming on my dick, and shuddered her release.

Then, I happily joined her.

thirty-eight

ELISE

As I caught my breath, my brain felt foggy. My thighs tightened, brushing the outside of Weston's, and I settled my gaze on him. He focused on me, subdued, with half-mast eyes.

He'd just filled me with his come. We were both coming down from our high, and I was about to puncture that exhilaration.

"How much?" I asked, forcing each bitter word off my tongue.

He blew his cheeks out. I slid off his cock and collapsed next to him with my back to the mattress. My chest felt heavy while I took in slow, deep breaths. My lungs constricted, burning with each exhale realizing what I'd just done.

I was so stupid.

"What?" he asked, turning on his side. He propped himself up on his elbow, his chest moving in and out as he rested his chin in the palm of his hand. His eyes penetrated mine while he waited for what was impending.

He wasn't ready for this conversation. Hell, I wasn't ready

for it. I dreaded bringing it up, but it had to happen. We needed to discuss this, or we could never move forward. There was no going on like it'd never happened. Me lying naked in his bed didn't mean we were back together and everything was forgotten.

His eyes dropped down to mine, flickering with gentleness and sympathy. He timidly reached out to push away the loose strands of hair falling in front of my eyes and played with it in his fingers. He shut his eyes, like he was afraid this was the last time he would touch me.

The sweet euphoria riding through me came to an afflicting crash. My stomach clamped with self-disgust.

He had hurt me, and what did I do? I jumped right back into his bed before deciding if I was forgiving him. I'd let him come inside me before we even resolved anything. My poor decision-making was still at its best.

"How much did he pay you?" I asked, the words slipping from my mouth, my tongue resisting their release.

"Please," he said, shaking his head. "Please don't bring him up in here." His tone was pleading. "Don't bring him up in here ever."

"Why?" I croaked, my blood temperature rising. "It needs to be talked about. You asked me to allow you to explain yourself and hear your side of the story. Now, start explaining."

He collapsed on his back, his elbow giving out. "Nuh-uh," he muttered, running his palm over his forehead, wiping away sweat droplets from our lovemaking. "Not here."

"Yes, here," I said through clenched teeth with a scowl.

I was suddenly feeling insecure and way too exposed. I bent forward, snatched the blanket at our ankles, and jerked it up my body.

"Tell me right now, or I'm getting up from this bed, calling

Vincent, and asking him to come get me. If you don't tell me why you did it, we're done. No more chances."

He sighed loudly, and the bed caved in when he smacked his arms down. "I don't want him in here, goddammit!" He turned back around to stare at me. "This is our place. I don't want him to have the privilege of tainting our bedroom. I don't want that monster brought up here."

He wasn't going to answer. He'd lied.

"This should've never happened." I draped my arm over my eyes in regret. "I shouldn't be here."

Stupid, stupid me. I should've never left with him. I damn sure shouldn't have slept with him. He was lying again. He'd played recklessly with my heart, leading me on like what he'd done was no big deal. I shouldn't be lying in his bed, but I couldn't find the strength to get up and walk away from him.

"This should've happened," he said.

I frowned when my arm was lifted and his face hovered above mine. I turned my head to the side, refusing eye contact.

"I'm not supposed to be here." I squeezed my eyes shut to hold back the fresh tears. "We're not supposed to be together."

He leaned forward and started to kiss away the tears falling down my cheeks. After he cleared each one, he kissed my damp lips. "You're supposed to be here."

I shook my head violently.

"There's no breaking us, baby."

"You hurt me."

"I did," he said in shame. "And I hate myself for it. I hate myself for being the person who caused you pain. I wanted to be the one who made you happy, the one you trusted, your hero, and I failed you. For that, I'm so sorry. If you give me another chance, I promise you that I will never let you down again."

He wasn't disputing what he'd done or giving me excuses to

justify his actions. He knew what he had done was wrong and owned up to it. More than anything else he could've said, the sadness in his voice and the look in his eyes told me he regretted it.

"I don't know if I can trust you again," I said.

A heavy numbness invaded me. I wanted to let him back in, fall back into his arms, and go back to when we were happy. But as much as I ached for that, it couldn't happen. There was no forgetting what happened, no matter how much time has passed. It would haunt us forever.

"Let me prove it to you," he begged. "I've never given you a reason to doubt my feelings for you. I know I made a bad decision. I should've been honest with you about it, but not once have I hurt you after we reconnected ... since I've been in love with you."

"Then, tell me," I whispered.

His chest expanded before he let out a rush of air. "Come on then." He got up, pulled a pair of shorts on, and came to me with his hand held out. "We're not doing it in here."

I wrapped the blanket tighter around me and let him pull me up. He followed me into the living room. I crashed on the couch, my back hitting the armrest, and he fell next to me.

"It was the day after we met," he said. "I went to the director about you telling me you were raped. He insisted I let it go, saying I wasn't the first therapist to come to him with that information, and every time he investigated it, it wasn't true. There was no supporting evidence to back up what you said."

"Of course, he said that," I replied, rolling my eyes. "I'm sure he had been paid off too."

He gave me a look.

"Sorry. Go on."

"He called me into his office the next morning, and your father was waiting for me. He reiterated everything I'd already been told. He told me you lied for attention and your false accusations would only hurt and break up families."

He was right. Not about the false accusations, but about tearing families apart. If my secret had come out then, Weston's family would've been over long ago.

He shook his head. "Wow. Now that I say it aloud, I was an idiot for believing it."

"He offered you money to keep your mouth shut, and you caved."

He nodded and frowned. "And I hate myself for it."

"How much?"

Pain crossed his face. "One hundred thousand."

"One hundred thousand dollars?" I yelped.

Repugnance filled my throat. My father had spent that much money to save his reputation. And so I'd remain a pawn in his sick game.

I bowed my head. "Thank you for being honest with me."

"I regret it every day of my life. I know it's not an excuse, but I was young and dumb. I wanted to do my job and help people."

I wasn't exactly content with his answer. It was long overdue, but I was relieved I'd finally gotten the truth.

"Okay," I said softly. "So, where do we go from here?"

"That's your call."

My call. My call to decide if I wanted to get dressed and make a run for it or stay and see where this would go. My call as to whether I wanted to open my heart back up and trust him again.

"I don't want to lose us, but I can't just run back to you and act like this never happened." I paused and then signaled between us. "This can't happen for a while. I need some time."

He grabbed my hands, cupping them in his. "Anything. You're calling the shots. Whatever makes you happy makes me happy."

He stopped as if something had dawned on him. "Unless you being happy is not being with me, no, it doesn't make me happy. I'll accept it, but I won't be happy. You've pretty much turned my world upside down. I told you I wanted Wale's death to mean something, and that's happened. He brought us together."

We were both giving each other something we needed. He helped people, including me.

"Baby steps." I gave him a small smile. "But I'm not leaving."

He wrapped his hand around my neck, bringing my lips to his. "Thank God. I missed you."

"I missed you too."

He clapped his hands. "Now, moving on. Let's talk about the topic of you loving me."

I clenched the blanket around me tighter. *Me and my big mouth.* "I don't know what you're talking about." I tried to hold back a smile but failed miserably. I couldn't hide my emotions around him.

"You do." A big, obnoxious smile spread across his face. "And don't try to deny it."

I shook my head, letting a smile pop. "One should not be held responsible for what they say when naked and on the verge of coital bliss."

He threw his head back, laughing. "Coital bliss? Really?"

I smacked his shoulder. "Yes, really. So, you can't hold anything I say or do during moments of pleasure against me. I'm like a loose cannon when you're devouring me. You use your tongue, and all of ... that"—I grow red, throwing my hands out to gesture toward his bare chest and then his cock—"makes me go crazy."

"I will use it against you when it works in my favor. Remember that."

I chirped up, faking a glare, "I believe I also said I hated you."

"Nuh-uh. You said you hated me when tearing my clothes off my body and when your hand was wrapped around my cock. You love me," he teased. "Don't be embarrassed about it. The feeling is mutual, love. But I'm sure you already know that."

I believed him. As crazy as it sounded, I knew he loved me because he looked at me the same way my father stared at pictures of my mother. My father might've been a horrible person, but he was head over heels in love with my mother. Even the darkest and most twisted people had a place inside them that was capable of love when they found the right person to fill that hollow part of their soul.

"I've never had anyone love me before," I said.

Men had proclaimed their love and infatuation to me before, but they were never real. Hell, I hadn't even been sure love existed until Weston. I didn't think people believed in love until they actually fell in love. You didn't know it was real until it hit you in the face and you realized you didn't feel complete without the other.

He wrapped his arms around me. "Then, I'm honored to be your first and last, and I promise you that you'll never lose my heart."

thirty-nine

ELISE

I blew out a breath of exhaustion as I clutched the two grocery bags in my arms and walked down the hallway. Since staying in my apartment and making weekly trips to the grocery store, I'd developed anxiety that my poor coordination would get to me and I'd drop something. The bag would bust open at my feet, and everything inside would fly in all directions.

And it happened.

Boom!

Like I could sense him, a bag fell from my grasp and smashed onto the carpeted floor. I gasped as items rolled down the hallway in what seemed like slow motion. Of course, my father had found me. He kicked a leg out and stopped a can with the sole of his Italian leather shoe.

"You need to get the hell out of here," I said coldly "Or I'm calling the cops."

"I only want to talk," he said, his dark eyes swallowing me in.

He was slouched, sitting against the wall, and sat at my

front door. There was no way I could avoid going near him if I wanted in my apartment.

"I don't want to talk," I snapped. "So, I'd appreciate it if you got your ass up and away from my door. Don't come back here again."

He held his hand out. "Five minutes. *Five minutes.* I'm not going to hurt you."

"Go away," I snarled, my harsh words surprising us both. "Did you think I'd be happy to see you and invite you in for a cup of tea?"

"I'm sorry."

The world stood still, and I grew light-headed. In my years of knowing this depraved man, he'd never—*not even once*—apologized for anything. I had been convinced he was incapable of remorse.

"You want penance?" I asked, my voice getting louder. "For which part?"

We both jumped when old lady Martha threw open her door. She popped her head out of her doorway to give us both a frigid glare.

Martha was apparently the only tenant in the complex who could make noise. We couldn't raise our voices or have the volume on our TV too high, but it was completely passable for her to blare Elvis Presley on repeat at seven in the morning.

I rolled my eyes, waving my hand at her to go back inside. The walls shook as her door slammed shut.

"Get up," I said, moving forward and kicking his leg roughly.

He wouldn't leave until I agreed to talk to him. He'd hold our conversation in the hallway and scream out my dirty laundry for all my neighbors to hear if I didn't let him in.

I rested my bag on my knee. "Five minutes, you hear me? If you do anything stupid, I'm calling the cops."

"I won't hurt you," he muttered.

He didn't bring himself up until I opened my door and walked inside. He picked up the remainder of my fallen groceries in the hallway and followed me.

I tossed my bag onto the counter, keeping a steady distance from him.

"Start talking," I demanded.

His appearance wasn't any different. There were no hints of him being a father grieving the loss of contact with his daughter—the only family he had left.

He inhaled a deep breath and shoved his hands into his pockets. "I thought I could try to get you back."

I gripped the edge of my countertop and told myself I would not scream at him until he was done, until after I heard his bullshit excuses.

"I thought if I came here, I could convince you to come home, but I realize it might be too late. You're done with me, aren't you?"

I drummed my fingers along the countertop, refusing eye contact. I wasn't sure if it was because I was too disgusted to face him or if I was too scared. "Sure am."

He nodded in defeat, shocking me. Clint Parks never gave up easily, and I wondered what he had up his sleeve.

"I was drunk," he finally stammered. "That night ... I was drunk."

"Are you serious?" I asked, baffled. "Is that the best cop-out you have for trying to rape your daughter? Is that your best defense for repeatedly hurting your own flesh and blood?"

He shook his head violently while scrambling for the right way to fix this. He was a smooth talker who bantered off hollow words. He was going to find a way to talk his way out of this. "It's not a justification for what I did. There's no excuse for that, baby girl. I'm so ashamed, but I would've never done that while sober." He slammed a finger in the center of his chest. "You know that, Elise. You know me. I'm your father! I've been there for you since the very start."

I stared at him in disgust. "You're absolutely right, Father. I do know you, and I know you're a horrible person. You're a monster, and I thank God every single day that I got away from you."

"Forgive me," he pleaded.

"Forgive you?" I repeated, losing patience. "Forgive you for pimping me out?"

He dodged a bag of chips thrown his way.

"Or do you want me to forgive you for repeatedly shipping me away to some mental institution for no valid reason?" I snorted. "Or better yet, do you want me to forgive you for trying to rape me? Oh, and let's not forget the scene you made at Weston's, where you made me come face-to-face with my first fucking rapist!"

I snatched up a glass and launched it across the room. "So, you tell me, what exactly are you apologizing for?"

He slammed his eyes shut. "All of it."

"You think a simple apology is going to fix all that? Nothing —and I mean, nothing—will ever get me to forgive you. You are nothing to me. You will never be forgiven. I am done with you."

"But I'm your father!"

"We might share blood, but you're not my father." I let out a deep breath and shook my head. "I could go on and on, but I'm done. You've exhausted me in every physical and emotional way possible. I want to move on, and if you care for me like you say, you'll give that to me. Turn around, walk out the door, and never come back. Let me be happy."

"But I can't lose you," he said, his voice strained. "You're all I have left."

"You lost me a long time ago."

I could see the hurt in his eyes. He never thought this day would come. He never thought he'd lose control of me.

"Is this good-bye?"

"This is. Stay away from me. Let me go. Please don't make me run."

forty

ELISE

"Wow, this is amazing." I stomped off my boots, pulled off my gloves, and scanned the place.

The building Weston had brought me to paint was finished. The stairs were stained to match the floor, and the doors had been replaced with new ones. Freshly painted mailboxes were labeled with apartment numbers.

"So, are we going to be painting?" I asked, raising a brow. "Because I want to make it clear that I'm totally up for that again."

He unwrapped his scarf before shaking his head and chuckling. "Yes, my love, we're going to be painting today—along with a few other activities." He broke the distance between us, circled his arm around my waist, and squeezed my side.

"And what kinds of things?" I questioned, leaning back against him, my ass grazing his cock.

The hairs on the back of my neck stood up, and shivers stretched over my skin with excitement. We hadn't had sex since the night we'd left the museum. I regretted telling him I wanted to take things slow.

"Yo, Doc!"

I glanced up to find a man at the top of the stairs with a tiny girl standing by his side. The man grabbed the girl's hand, gripping it tightly, and they both hopped down each stair.

"Good timing," the man said, stopping in front of us as Weston moved to stand next to me. "I was on my way down here to mail rent but might as well give it to you now."

I jerked my head to the side, eyeing Weston curiously when he took the envelope from the man, the word *rent* scribbled across it in red crayon.

"I appreciate you giving me an extra week," the man went on. "My check was a few days short because of the snow."

My stomach dropped. His face was weary, he appeared sleep and shower deprived. His face was unshaven. His boots and coat were stained and ripped. I switched my gaze to the girl, noticing the great condition of her furry pink boots and coat. Her hair was brushed and pulled into pigtails on each side of her head.

Weston slipped the envelope into his pocket. "No worries, Glen," he said, smacking the guy on the shoulder. "I'm happy to help." Reaching down, he ruffled the girl's hair, resulting in a front-tooth-missing smile. "You have to take care of this little one."

The girl's attention went to Weston when Glen squeezed her tiny hand. "I love my boots, Mr. Weston. Pink is my favorite color," she told him eagerly. "Thank you so much."

My heart melted as I watched their interaction.

"You're very welcome," Weston replied. "I'm glad you like them."

"Well, we're off to the babysitter," Glen told us, guiding the girl toward the door, and they both gave us a wave. He stopped before walking out. "And if you ever need anything repaired around here, I owe you one."

Weston nodded. "I appreciate that. You two stay warm."

"So, you own this place?" I asked, biting at my lower lip.

Weston nodded, his eyes falling to the floor. "I do."

"Why didn't you tell me?"

He shrugged. "I was going to eventually."

I clicked my tongue against the roof of my mouth. "You seem to have a knack for waiting to tell me things *eventually*."

He blinked at me.

"Why don't you live here if you own it?"

He reached out and grabbed my hand, and I stumbled a few times as he pulled me up the stairs. "I'll explain everything to you."

"*Eventually*," I added, upping my pace to keep up with him.

He opened the front door to apartment 2B, allowing me to go in first.

"My lease isn't up on my apartment for another eight months, and it's closer to my office," he explained, shutting the door.

He grabbed my arm, his body crowding mine while he unzipped my coat. He pulled it off, arm by arm, and then tossed it onto the couch alongside his.

I slipped off my shoes. "Then, why did you buy it if you can't live in it?"

I moved around the studio, observing the paintings again, being drawn in, even after seeing them before. The place was still as spectacular as ever ... maybe even more now that we had memories to go along with them.

"I did volunteer work at a shelter in the city," he explained, grabbing me around the side of the waist and dragging me around the room. "After I paid off my loans, I decided to help some of the families there. I found this place in foreclosure and got a great deal on it." His voice lowered, as he knew I'd catch on to how he'd afforded. "It's hard for homeless people to get jobs because they don't have an address or a phone number. So, I provide them with a few free months of rent, help them with furniture and a phone, and then they pay rent when they get a job and save up."

"At least the money went to good use," I muttered, attempting to pull away from him, but he constricted his grip on me.

We might've cleared the air by him telling me what he'd done, but that didn't mean it still didn't hurt when it was brought up. I'd always be affected by the deal they'd made.

I squirmed, feeling his breath against my neck, and his mouth dropped to my ear.

"Let's not ruin this. I brought you here because I want to give you something," he whispered.

"And what is that?" I asked, running my hand up his side and then caressing his cheek as he stood behind me.

He kissed my neck, his soft lips making me needy for more, and then turned me around before pulling away. He walked across the room, grabbed a painting from the wall, and handed it to me.

"Did you buy this from your friend?" I asked, staring down at the picture.

It was the one I'd fallen in love with the last time we were here. I stared at it closely, remembering how I'd connected with it and how much progress I'd made from not being that woman in hiding anymore.

"Technically, I bought it from myself," he said, his eyes penetrating mine, like he was waiting for a reaction.

"So, this was already yours?" I asked.

He shook his head, a smile tugging at his lips. "No, I painted it."

His hand dashed forward to catch the canvas when it dropped from my grip. He secured it in his hands, holding it against his chest.

"What do you mean, you painted it?"

"I'm the person who painted this." He held it up. "I'm the artist."

"So, there was no friend?"

He shook his head, and I tossed an arm out.

"Seriously? You made that up too? Why didn't you tell me?" I paused, letting the fact that he'd painted a portrait of me before we even saw each other again sink in. "I'm trying to decide if that's the creepiest ... or the most romantic thing anyone has ever done for me."

He forced out a laugh. "And I'm praying you go with romantic." He continued to wait for my response, but my mouth slammed shut while I ran everything through my mind.

"Look," he rushed out, noticing my indecision, "I didn't paint this picture with a fantasy of you. I painted it because of your story. This is how I saw you when we met, and it stuck with me. I couldn't get you out of my mind, so I found a way to clear my thoughts of you."

I took a step forward, my eyebrows rising in amusement. "So, I've been on your mind for years?" I asked flirtatiously.

"I didn't see it that way then, but now that I think about it, yes."

I snatched the painting from his hand, running my fingers along the woman's—or *my*—face, and admired all the shapes and colors. "You're talented, so I'm going to go with romantic."

"Really?"

"It's romantic. It's hot. It might be borderline stalker, but because I love you, I guess that makes it okay."

I carefully placed the painting down on the floor and grabbed his hand to yank him forward toward the couch. His sweater was itchy against my palms when I shoved him down onto the couch, his back bumping against the cushions. I hiked up a leg, my foot resting next to him, and quickly straddled his lap.

He gasped, and his breathing grew rapidly when I started to rock against him. Excitement wound through me when I felt his growing arousal, hidden underneath his jeans, rub against me.

"So, did you bring me here to see the painting, or did you bring me here to get me naked?" I asked, locking eyes with him.

He shivered as I ran my tongue along his lower lip and grabbed my waist, holding me in place so I couldn't move. "I brought you here to show you the painting and see your reaction."

I grinned, rolling my hips in a circle so he'd loosen his grip. "And how do you feel about this reaction, Doctor?"

"I love this reaction," he said, roughly dipping me down onto him. "This is definitely one I was hoping for."

I yelped, jumping up when his hand connected with my ass, and he pushed me down against his hard cock again.

I lowered my face to his neck, sliding the tip of my nose against his skin, noticing the goose bumps erupt. I slid my tongue against them, tasting his skin.

"As much as I love your art, I like the work we make a little bit better," I told him, yanking his sweater over his head and watching the goose bumps expand.

"I completely agree," he said, pulling off my top and throwing it across the room. "Nothing out there competes with the beauty of your naked body sprawled out and ready for me. I think that will be my next painting."

"I think I like that idea."

A hand went to each side of his face, holding him in place while we locked lips. His tongue slid against mine. He used one finger to unbutton my jeans and frowned when I stopped him from sinking his hand underneath my panties. I wanted his hand on my pussy, but my mouth was watering for something else.

I unsnapped his jeans, taking them and his boxers with me as I crawled down his body and dropped to my knees. I wasted no time bringing out his hard cock and wrapping my hand around it, salivating as I took it in with bewildered eyes.

I pulled my lips together and watched him twitch when I blew out a heavy breath along the top of his length. He shivered, his cock stirring and growing harder. I glanced up at him, noticing his mouth open and his head tilted back.

I slid the tie from my wrist, pulled my hair up, and took him in my mouth. My tongue wrapped around him, eliciting a moan from his throat as I worked him in and out.

"Up," he rasped, leaning forward, grabbing me underneath my armpits, and throwing me on the couch next to him.

I stayed still while he undressed me, and then he shed his pants from his ankles. His eyes drank me in, sitting on the couch, and I waited for him to tell me what to do next.

"Turn around," he demanded. "On all fours."

I did as I had been told, bending down on my hands and knees with my ass facing the air. He positioned himself behind me, and I bucked forward when he smacked my ass. A chilly finger ran along the inside of my thigh and then moved up to my slit.

"Already dripping for me," he groaned out, putting a finger inside me.

My head flew back, my hips colliding with his arm, needing more. He took his excruciating time, teasing me, fingering me slowly, like he wanted to drag this out all day long.

"Fuck me already," I gasped.

He laughed, his finger pumping harder. I struggled against him, ready to pull away and jump on his cock, but he wouldn't let me. My breathing hitched when I felt his cock pressing against my pussy, and he paused, driving me insane while I whimpered in front of him, begging him to fuck me until he did.

My head bowed, watching his cock penetrate me over and over again.

I trusted this man.

I loved this man.

He'd changed my life.

He'd saved me.

epilogue

ELISE

To say my life had changed drastically was an understatement. Since I'd left my father, I'd gotten my driver's license, started classes at the community college, and began interning at the rape crisis center. I never imagined how deeply it'd impact me helping other women who'd struggled with the same trauma I had. It helped me heal as I helped them heal. Just like Weston, I wanted to help people.

Even though it'd been years and I'd been scared, I turned my father into the police. There wasn't enough evidence to press charges against him, but the story went viral. People saw the accusations. The board of his company forced him to step down, and I hadn't heard from him since.

The other men who raped me, including Weston's father, were arrested. Not all of them were charged, but they still had that attachment to their name. Just like my father—they lost their careers, families, and reputations. I'd been terrified of Weston hating me when I decided to turn his father in, but he'd been by my side, holding my hand while I told the police everything.

But Weston wasn't the only one I had to worry about hating me for turning his father in.

I feared what his family would think of me.

His mother divorced his father, and the family cut off all communication with him. But that didn't mean they wouldn't hold a grudge toward me.

Weston swore his family held no ill-will, but I asked him for time. He understood and said whenever I was ready. He wanted me to experience what it was like to have a family at your side.

And the time had come.

My hands were sweaty when Weston pulled into the gated neighborhood and parked his car in the drive of a large Tudor home. The yard was spectacularly landscaped, and a child's bicycle was near the front porch. A white SUV was parked in front of us with a Columbia sticker on the back window.

"You okay?" Weston asked.

My nerves were on fire. "Yes, but no."

"I swear, everything will be okay I wouldn't put you in this situation if I knew my family wouldn't be kind to you." Weston grabbed my hands together and kissed them. "If you feel uncomfortable at any time, we'll leave."

I swallowed hard and nodded as he released me before stepping out of the car. He opened the door for me, grabbed my hand to interlace our fingers, and we took slow steps to the front door. I prayed to God I didn't pass out.

"There they are!" a woman shouted as soon as the door flew open. She rushed toward me and practically dragged us through the front door. "I've been waiting to meet you, Elise."

I could feel the anxiety coming. I was meeting the mother of the man I was in love with, which was expected in a new couple. What wasn't expected 1 was that she also happened to be the ex-wife of my rapist, who I'd put in jail.

"Mom, be easy on her," Weston warned.

She didn't listen to him. Instead, she grabbed me by my stiff shoulders to hold me at a distance, and I stayed frozen when she threw her arms around me.

"I am being easy on her," she argued, pulling away from me. "But I'm so excited, so don't ruin this for me."

I gave her a weak smile as she stood in front of me. Weston's mother was beautiful. Her strawberry-blonde hair was pulled into a low bun. She appeared casual for dinner, wearing a white button-up shirt and a black cotton skirt that hit her ankles. I wasn't sure how someone so sweet could've been married to such a monster.

I spotted Julia heading in our direction, and she waved to me with a smile.

"I'm glad you two could make it," Julia said.

"Dang, dude, I thought they were lying when they said you had a girlfriend—and a pretty one at that," a guy said, walking into the room with a small girl on his shoulders. His brown hair was combed back, and he wore a polo shirt, jeans, and loafers.

He reminded me of Vincent. The girl on his shoulders, grinning from ear to ear, couldn't have been any older than five or six.

"Funny, Bruce," Weston told the guy. "Don't make me have my sister divorce you."

"Yeah, right," he muttered, bending forward and helping the girl down.

"He plays with people's minds for a living. I'm sure if he wanted to, he could have me rethinking our entire relationship and have me packing your bags ... or throwing them out into the front lawn," Julia said, cutting in.

"It's nice to see you love me so much," Bruce grumbled, fake glaring at his wife.

"See," Weston said, tilting his head toward his sister. "Don't mess with me, man."

Weston hunched over when Julia rammed her arm into his stomach.

"Just kidding, pretty boy," Julia joked. "You think too highly of yourself."

"Yeah, she's never leaving this," Bruce fired back, motioning toward his body.

"Dear God," Julia said, shaking her head. "Our daughter is right there."

"I love my daddy!" the little girl yelled.

She wrapped her arms around his legs, and he smiled brightly, telling her he loved her more.

"This is Elise," Weston said, finally having the chance to introduce me. "And this is my mother, Laura. My sister, Julia, who you've already met, and her husband, Bruce." He picked up the small girl and kissed her cheek. "And this is my favorite little niece, Addie."

"I'm your only niece," Addie said, shoving his shoulder.

She jumped down from him and wrapped her arms around my legs. I scanned the room, not sure what to do, so I patted her head.

"You're pretty!" Addie squealed. "My Uncle Weston talks about you all the time!"

My heart warmed, and my shoulders settled.

No one hated me.

I watched in awe as they joked around with each other. It was amazing to witness something so ... functional and normal. This family truly and genuinely loved each other, and they were offering me a spot in their happiness. They were giving me the family I wished I'd had, and as nervous as I was to take a seat at the table, I knew it would be okay.

I took a deep breath, trying my best to hide my unease, and shot them all a wave.

"Welcome to the family, Elise. We're so glad to have you here. I've been dying to meet the girl my son can't stop talking about," Laura said, smiling wide. "Dinner is ready, so let's eat."

Weston stopped me before we followed the others into the kitchen. "You good?" he asked, clasping my face in his hands, and his eyes met mine.

I nodded and smiled. "I am. I'm better than I've been in a long time."

He kissed me. "We both are, and it only gets better from here, love. Now, let's go hang out with our family."

Weston had given me something I'd never thought I'd have. He gave me love, freedom, appreciation, and a family. He made me feel like I was worth something—even when I didn't believe in myself. He'd saved me from my unhappiness, and I couldn't wait to spend the rest of my life with him, creating our happiness together.

We helped each other heal and grew our love from there.

Weston had taken my reckless heart in his careful hands and saved me. I couldn't wait for what our future held.

also by charity ferrell

ONLY YOU SERIES

(each book can be read as a standalone)

Only Rivals

Only Coworkers

BLUE BEECH SERIES

(each book can be read as a standalone)

Just A Fling

Just One Night

Just Exes

Just Neighbors

Just Roommates

Just Friends

TWISTED FOX SERIES

(each book can be read as a standalone)

Stirred

Shaken

Straight Up

Chaser

Last Round

MARCHETTI MAFIA SERIES

(each book can be read as a standalone)

Gorgeous Monster

Gorgeous Prince

STANDALONES

Bad For You

Beneath Our Faults

Beneath Our Loss

Pop Rock

Pretty and Reckless

Wild Thoughts

RISKY DUET

Risky

Worth The Risk

about the author

Charity Ferrell is a USA Today and Wall Street Journal best-selling author of the Twisted Fox and Blue Beech series. She resides in Indianapolis, Indiana with her fiancé and two fur babies. She loves writing about broken people finding love while adding humor and heartbreak along with it. Angst is her happy place.

When she's not writing, she's making a Starbucks run, shopping online, or spending time with her family.

Made in United States
Orlando, FL
13 October 2022

23276675R10157